# Dark Calling

BOOK NINE

THE DEMONATA

*Other titles by*

# DARREN SHAN

## THE DEMONATA

1 Lord Loss*
2 Demon Thief*
3 Slawter*
4 Bec*
5 Blood Beast*
6 Demon Apocalypse*
7 Death's Shadow
8 Wolf Island

## THE SAGA OF DARREN SHAN

1 Cirque Du Freak*
2 The Vampire's Assistant*
3 Tunnels of Blood*
4 Vampire Mountain
5 Trials of Death
6 The Vampire Prince
7 Hunters of the Dusk
8 Allies of the Night
9 Killers of the Dawn
10 The Lake of Souls
11 Lord of the Shadows
12 Sons of Destiny

**Also available on audio*

# DARREN SHAN

# Dark Calling

HarperCollins *Children's Books*

Answer the call of the dark at
www.darrenshan.com

First published in hardback in Great Britain by HarperCollins *Children's Books* 2009
HarperCollins *Children's Books* is a division of HarperCollins *Publishers* Ltd
77-85 Fulham Palace Road, Hammersmith, London, W6 8JB

www.harpercollins.co.uk

1



ISBN-13: 978 0 00 726044 7



Printed and bound in Great Britain by
Clays Ltd, St Ives plc

*For:*

Bas — you love it when I call!

*OBEs (Order of the Bloody Entrails) to:*

Sam "the snapper" White

Rachel Wasdyke — demon mistress of New Orleans

Tom Woodhead – in a word – Sligstatic!!!

*Hallowed hollerer:*

Stella Paskins

*Greek chorus:*

the Christopher Little choir

# TURN AROUND, BRIGHT EYES

→A small, wiry, scorpion-shaped demon with a semi-human face drives its stinger into my right eye. My eyeball pops and gooey streaks flood down my cheek. In complete agony, I scream helplessly, but worse is to come. The demon spits into the empty socket. At first I think it's just phlegm, but then dozens of tiny *things* start to wriggle in the space where my eye once swam. As I fill with confused horror, teeth or claws dig into the bone around my ruined eye. Whatever the mini-monsters are, they're trying to tunnel through to my brain.

Beranabus roars, "*Kernel!*" and tries to grab me, but I wheel away from him as insanity and pain claim me. I whip around, flailing, shrieking, wild. The demon strikes again and punctures my left eye. Darkness consumes me. I'm in hell.

→A lifetime later, someone picks me up from where I've fallen and drags me forward. It might be Beranabus or Grubbs, or maybe it's Lord Loss. I don't know or care. All I can focus on is the blind, hellish pain.

I pull away from the person or demon and run from the madness, but crash into something hard. I fall, moaning and screaming, but not crying — I no longer have eyes to weep with. The creatures which were spat into my eyes are munching on my brain now. I try to scrape them out with my fingers, but that just adds to the torment.

Then magic sears through my ruined sockets. The things in my head burn and drop away. The pain lessens. I sigh blissfully and slump unconscious.

→I dream of the end of the world. Everything comes apart and everyone perishes. The universe warps and twists upon itself. In my dream, I float as a spirit through panels of light. I don't know how I see the lights without eyes, but I do. There are others — Grubbs, Beranabus, a girl. I slot the patches of light together and we sail from one window to another. Peaceful. No pain. I'm at ease. In my element. Master of the lights.

Maybe this is heaven. Constructing and passing through an endless series of windows. An eternal, beautiful, cosmic light show. I'll settle for that. Anything's better than torture, blindness and micro-demons feasting on my brain.

→Heaven doesn't last. I wasn't dreaming. The destruction was real. The lights fade and I find myself back on Earth. Blind as ever. Pain muted by magic, but hovering, waiting for its chance to kick back in. Turns out the creatures in my eyes were *maggots*.

No time for panic or self-pity. Beranabus drops a bombshell — we've travelled through time. I'm part of a magical weapon, the Kah-Gash. Grubbs is another part. By linking with the third component, the ghost of a dead girl, we took our doomed world into the past to avert demonic conquest. Now we have to fight again or it will all have been for nothing.

→In a cave. Blindly battling Spine, the scorpion demon. I have the horrible beast pinned to a stalagmite. I'm pounding him with my fists, over and over. Without warning he melts away and I'm left standing in a puddle of sticky blood, frowning sightlessly.

I later learn that I've been cheated out of my revenge by a girl called Bec who's returned to life after sixteen hundred years. She drives Lord Loss back to his own foul realm. Job done.

→We return to the universe of the Demonata. Grubbs comes with us, but Bec stays behind. I'm surprised Beranabus leaves her. She's part of the Kah-Gash. By uniting us, he could wield the power of the ancient weapon and destroy the Demonata. But he's afraid. The Kah-Gash made an independent decision to reverse time. Beranabus isn't sure whether that was a conscious act of mercy or a random reaction. He doesn't want to press ahead, worried the weapon might side with the demons next time and wipe out mankind.

I'm stronger in the universe of magic. I numb my pain and set to work on building a new set of eyes. I'm not sure that I can. Magic varies from person to person. We all have different capabilities. Some can restore a missing limb or organ. Others can't. You never know until you try.

Thankfully I'm one of those who can. With only the slightest guidance from Beranabus I construct a pair of sparkling blue eyes. I build them from the rear of my sockets outwards, repairing severed nerve endings, linking them with the growing globes, letting the orbs expand to fill the gaps.

I keep my eyelids shut for a minute when the eyes are complete, afraid I won't be able to see anything when I open them. I hardly breathe, heart beating fast, contemplating a life of darkness, the worst punishment I can imagine.

Then Beranabus stamps on my foot. I yell and my

eyes snap open. I turn on the magician angrily, raising a fist, but stop when I see his cunning smile. I *see* it.

"You looked like an idiot with your eyes shut," Beranabus grunts.

"You're a bully," I pout, then laugh with relief and hug him. He's laughing too, but Grubbs isn't. The teenager glares at us. He's lost his brother and abandoned his uncle and home. He's in no mood to give a stuff about my well-being. But that's fine. Right now I can't sympathise with him either. All I care about is that I can see. I relish my new eyes, drinking in the sights of the demon world.

I'm so happy, it's several hours before I realise I can see more than before, that my new eyes have opened up a wonder of the universe previously hidden from me.

→I've always been able to see patches of light which are invisible to everybody else. For years I thought they were products of my imagination, that I was slightly (*light*ly) crazy. Then I learnt they were part of the realm of magic. I have a unique talent. I can manually slot the patches together and create windows between universes, far faster than anyone else.

I use my talent to help Beranabus save the world from demons. The magician has been around for thousands of years and has spent much of that time patrolling the demon universe, protecting humanity from its savage, nightmarish hordes. Although demons have limitless galaxies of their own, they long to cross over — they love killing humans.

Beranabus stops them. He ensures no tunnels are built between universes, holds the demon armies in check, prevents mass crossings. I assist him. My gift allows us to zip from one part of the demon universe to another and track down just about any demon we want.

I thought I might not be able to see the lights with my new eyes, but they work the same way as my original pair. I can still see the multicoloured patches, and when I think of a specific place, person or thing, some of the lights flash and I can slot them together to create a window. In fact I can do it quicker than before and my powers on Earth are greater than they were. Where I used to struggle to open windows on my own world, now I can do it swiftly and easily.

But now there are other lights. At first I thought they were illusionary specks, that my new eyes weren't working properly. But I soon realised the lights were real and fundamentally different to those I was familiar with. They're smaller, they change shape and their colours mutate. The regular lights never alter in size or shade, but these new patches grow and subside, bleed from one colour to another. A square pink panel can lengthen into a triangular blue patch, then gradually twist into an orange octagon, and so on.

They shimmer too. Their edges flicker like faulty fluorescent tubes. Sometimes creases run through them, like ripples spreading across the face of a pond.

I can't control the new lights. They ignore me when I try to manipulate them. In fact, if I start to get close, they glide away from me.

There aren't many of them, no more than twenty or thirty anywhere I go. But they worry me. There's something deeply unsettling about them. I initially thought that I was nervous of them just because they were new. But several weeks later, as I was trying to coax them nearer and link them up, they whispered to me.

I know it's ridiculous. Lights can't whisper. But I swear I heard a voice calling to me. It sounded like static to begin with, but then it came into focus, a single word repeated over and over. It's the same word the lights have been whispering to me ever since, softly, slyly, seductively.

*Come…*"

# A WORD IN YOUR EAR

→Beranabus unleashes a burst of magic and the gazelle-shaped demon we've been chasing stops in its tracks. The beast turns and snarls at us. It has the head of a human baby. Opening its mouth, it wails. The noise increases sharply and blood trickles from my ears and nose. I use magic to mute the demon's cry. Beranabus and Grubbs do the same and the three of us close in on the mewling monster.

When the demon realises it can't harm us with its harpy-like wailing, it falls silent and its look of hatred changes to one of fear. It knows who we are and what we want.

I hang back while Beranabus tortures the creature. I have a problem with demons that model themselves after babies or young children. I can't bring myself to hurt them, even though I know they've only stolen their human attributes.

I was a lonely child. Driven by unhappiness, I unintentionally tapped into my powers, kidnapped a demon and used magic to make it look like a baby. I convinced myself the changeling was my brother and I maintained the lie for ages. I was shattered when I learnt the truth. Demons like this one make me think of my "brother" Art and I go cold at the thought of harming them. Beranabus understands. He doesn't try to push me.

Grubbs rips off the demon's head. The baby-faced monster squeals with pain and terror, but doesn't die. In this universe of magic almost anything is possible. Physical dismemberment won't necessarily kill a demon. You need to use magic to finish it off.

Grubbs hates this life even more than I do. When I agreed to join Beranabus and devote myself to battling demons, I didn't have a better choice. My parents knew I wasn't normal, and though they loved me, they feared what I might do. I didn't have any friends. It was Beranabus or a life of isolation and loneliness.

Grubbs has an uncle who he loves like a father. He has lots of friends. He could have rejected his destiny. I'm not really sure why he didn't. Maybe it was the call of the Kah-Gash. Perhaps the weapon persuaded him to leave the human world and ride the demonic waves of this universe with Beranabus and me.

"The Shadow," Beranabus snarls, grabbing the baby's head from Grubbs and gouging out one of its snake-shaped eyes. "Tell us all you know and we'll let you go. Otherwise..." He moves his thumb over the creature's other eye.

The Shadow is our latest foe in a long line of monstrous opponents. Beranabus thinks it's our most dangerous enemy yet, but I'm not worried. I've seen all manner of unimaginable demons. In the early days I thought each was invincible. Every time we went up against one, I was sure we were doomed. But we always got the better of the beasts, pinpointed their weak spots, defeated them with cunning if brute force failed.

I know it's dangerous to assume we'll overcome every demon we go up against, but I can't help thinking that way. I'm sure the Shadow will fall to us when we face it, just like all the others. It's simply a matter of time, patience and violence.

Beranabus and Grubbs believe the Shadow is the herald of universal doom. They saw it in the cave when I was blind, a huge beast that seemed to be made from strips of shadow. They say it was deadlier than anything else we've fought. Maybe they're right. If I'd seen it, I might be trembling with fear too. But I don't think so. It's just another demon. We've fought and killed thousands of them since I joined Beranabus. How can this one be any different?

→We're hunting a flock of sheep-like demons. Each

boasts dozens of woolly heads dotted around its body, no eyes or ears, just large mouths full of sharp teeth. Beranabus hopes they know something about the Shadow, but I think he's scraping the bottom of the barrel.

The Shadow is as elusive as the name we've given it suggests. We've learnt almost nothing of the creature in all the time we've been trying to track it. We know it's gathering an army of demons, that it's promised to wipe out mankind and restore the universe to its original condition (whatever that means), but everything else about it is a mystery.

These minor demons – easy pickings for stronger members of the Demonata – won't provide us with any clues. We're wasting our time, as we've wasted it on so many worlds. We'll torture them, kill a few, then move on, no wiser than when we stepped through the window and set off in chase of the howling beasts.

As we close in on the flock, I sense a throbbing in the air nearby and draw to a halt.

"Come on!" Beranabus shouts. "Don't stop now. We–"

"A window's opening," I tell him, and excitement instantly gives way to panic.

"Start opening one of your own," Beranabus commands and steps in front of me, to protect me.

The tall, muscular Grubbs joins him. They think a demon is after us. But I know better. I've come to understand the lights more intimately than ever since I built my new pair of eyes. This is a window of human origin.

"Wait," I tell Beranabus. "It's not a demon. We have company."

Seconds later a window of orange light opens and two of Beranabus's Disciples step through. One's a beautiful, fiery woman called Meera Flame. I know the other one better, and shout his name with unconcealed joy. "Shark!"

"Been a long time, kid," the ex-soldier grins, shaking my hand as Grubbs and Meera hug close by. Beranabus is squinting at the newcomers suspiciously. He doesn't like surprises.

"What are you doing here?" I gasp.

"Came to catch the sun," Shark laughs, then casts his gaze over my bald, caramel-coloured head. "There's something different about your eyes."

"It's a long story." I smile broadly, still clutching him. We've spent long months in this foul universe and Beranabus and Grubbs are poor company. The unwelcome flames of loneliness have been burning hot inside me recently. I'm overjoyed to see my old friend, to escape the dark feelings for a few minutes. I know Shark must be the bearer of bad news, that he and Meera wouldn't have come unless things were serious, but for a few moments I block that out and pretend this is a social visit.

"Hi, Shark," Grubbs says.

Shark frowns. "Do I know you?"

"Grubbs Grady. We..." He pauses. "Dervish told me about you. I'm Grubbs, his nephew."

Shark nods. "I can see a bit of him in you. But you've got more hair. You're a lot taller too — what's Beranabus been feeding you?"

"Enough of the prattle," Beranabus snaps. "What's wrong?"

"We were attacked," Meera says. "I was at Dervish's. We–"

"Was it Lord Loss?" Beranabus barks. "Is Bec all right?"

"She's fine," Shark says.

"But Dervish..." Meera pauses, glancing nervously at Grubbs.

"He was alive when we left," Shark says as Grubbs freezes with fear.

"But in bad shape," Meera adds. "He had a heart attack."

"We have to go back," Grubbs says, darting for the window.

Shark stops him. "Hold on. We didn't come here directly. That leads to another demon world."

"Besides," I chip in, "if the demons are still at the house..."

"We weren't attacked by demons," Meera says. "They were... *Werewolves*."

That throws me. Does she mean werewolf-shaped demons? Then I recall the curse of the Gradys. Lots of teenagers in Grubbs's family turn into mindless, savage, wolf-like beasts.

Grubbs starts to tremble. Without waiting to be told, I turn, flex my fingers and focus, thinking of Dervish. Lights pulse around me — that means the ex-punk is still alive. I begin to open a window that will take us to him. Then, on second thoughts, I focus on Bec instead. As much as I like Dervish, the girl is more important. She's probably with him, but if not she must take priority. Dervish is only human. Bec – like me and Grubbs – is so much more.

→When a window of amber light opens, Beranabus rushes through, swiftly followed by Grubbs. "There are demons," I tell Shark and Meera, sensing their presence in the vibrations of the lights. "Are you guys ready to fight?"

"Always," Shark grins, cracking his knuckles.

Meera gulps, then grinds her teeth together and nods fiercely.

We cross.

I find myself in a hospital ward. Bec is lying on the floor. She looks like any normal girl, a bit smaller than most, but otherwise unremarkable. You would never guess from looking at her that she'd been dead for sixteen hundred years, or that this body wasn't originally hers.

Two demons are backing away from Bec. One is some sort of lizard hybrid. The other looks like an anteater with several snouts. One of its eyes is missing, blood and goo surrounding the empty socket. I suppress a shudder as Beranabus growls at the demons, "What do the pickings look like now?"

They turn and run. Shark bolts after them. Meera and I follow, leaving Beranabus and Grubbs to help Bec back to her feet. I wonder about Dervish, if he's still alive, but I've no time to dwell on that. Another window is open and the hospital has been flooded with magical energy, but I'm still nowhere near as strong here as I am in the demon universe. My power will dwindle. We need to deal with these monsters swiftly, and we have to be cautious. It's much easier to die on this world.

I spot the remains of a few babies as we pursue the demons. My stomach churns and I tear my gaze away from the tiny corpses. Even so, thoughts of Art flash through my mind. I fill with sorrow, then rage. They shouldn't have gone after the newborns. That was too cruel. I'm going to make them pay.

The demons burst out of the maternity ward and scuttle towards the stairs. Shark crouches, then propels himself forward, shooting through the air as if fired from a canon. He knocks the pair of demons aside and they crash into the wall on either side of the staircase. As they yelp with surprise and pain, Meera and I fall upon them. I take the lizard, leaving Meera to deal with the anteater.

It's a slimy little beast. It slithers around and lashes at me with a forked tongue. Drops of poison hit my eyes and sizzle. I use magic to transform the drops into water, then grab the demon's tongue and yank hard. It utters a choked scream. The tongue slips through my fingers. I follow it back into the demon's mouth, jamming my hand halfway down the lizard's throat. Taking a firmer hold of the tongue, I rip it loose and toss it away. Black blood gushes from the demon's mouth and its beady eyes roll wildly.

I let the demon drop, then pin it to the floor with one knee. I start tearing off scales, working my fingertips into the gaps, using magic to torment the demon. For a long time I didn't understand how Beranabus could butcher so nastily. As evil as demons are... as much as I accept the need to kill them... I couldn't condone torture. But my attitude has changed over the years. I've seen too many corpses.

Too many murdered babies. These monsters deserve all the agony we can put them through and a whole lot more on top.

Shark helps Meera finish off the anteater, then studies me as I work on the lizard.

"Need a hand, kid?"

"No," I pant.

The ex-soldier squats beside me and waits for me to look at him. "I know where you're coming from," he says quietly, "but we don't have time. There are others on the loose. They're still killing."

I sigh, then shoot a burst of magic into the lizard. It slumps and I rise. "Sorry."

"No need to apologise," Shark says. "Another time and place, I'd have joined in and we'd have had hours of fun."

"*Fun?*" Meera barks.

"Sure," Shark smiles. "You've got to get a buzz out of fighting. It'd be a hell of a life if you devoted your time to battle and didn't enjoy it."

"Anyone ever tell you you're a sicko?" Meera snorts.

"We're all the same," Shark protests. "I'm just more open about it. Killing demons is noble and necessary, blah blah blah. But it's a blast too. Right, Kernel?"

"Come on," I mutter, not wanting to engage in the debate, afraid I'd come down on Shark's side and not liking what that says about me. "Let's kill the rest of them before they slaughter more babies."

That sobers Shark and saps Meera of her indignation. Turning our backs on the dead demons, we go into killing mode and set off in search of monsters viler and more vicious than ourselves.

→We kill three more demons, then the mage who is keeping their window open. He's a thin, balding, middle-aged man in a cheap suit. He doesn't look evil. Most people who work for the Demonata don't. He shuts his eyes as we close in on him and doesn't cry out when Shark grabs his throat and crushes it. The nearby demons escape through the window to their own universe before it closes. We let them flee and get stuck into those left behind. Demons don't last long once a window shuts. Their bodies fall apart after a few minutes and they crumble away to dust. But they can still kill a lot of people during that time, so we afford them no mercy.

When the hospital's clean, we join the others on the roof. Bec, Dervish and Sharmila are there. Sharmila's legs have been cut off. Beranabus is working hard to patch her up. Dervish is sitting on a trolley, looking close to death. Meera goes to him immediately, to check that he's OK.

"I'll guard the staircase," Shark says. "Make sure we aren't taken by surprise."

"But the demons are gone," I frown.

"We have humans to worry about too," he snorts, then nods at Bec. "She'll tell you all about it."

And she does, swiftly and clearly. It's a disturbing story. First I learn that an old enemy – once a friend – has returned from beyond the grave. Juni Swan, who I first knew as Nadia Moore, has come back to life in a new, mutated form.

I'm always torn when I think of Nadia/Juni. She was a bitter but kind young woman when we first met. She saved my life in Lord Loss's realm when I fell into a river of lava. She told me then to be wary of her if we ever met again, that she served the demon master now and I should think of her as a foe. But I find it hard to hate her. She's a person who lost her way. She didn't seek out evil — she got sucked into it. I pity her as much as I fear and mistrust her.

Bec describes the attack on Dervish's home in Carcery Vale. Werewolves broke in, supported by humans with guns. She tells us she has a curious gift — she can absorb the memories of anyone she touches. One of the werewolves was a Grady. Its parents turned it over to the Lambs – family executioners – to dispose of. But the Lambs kept the beast alive and they or some other group subsequently used it as a weapon.

We discuss this troubling turn of events. Grubbs is

more worked up than the rest of us — he hates the thought of his relatives being manipulated. Bec thinks Lord Loss masterminded the attack, that he knows she's part of the Kah-Gash. Beranabus agrees, then tells me to open a window. Dervish and Sharmila won't last long in this universe. They need magic to survive.

I'm glad to set to work on the window because I need magic too. My eyes are burning. It was bad as soon as I set foot on this world, but since the demons' window closed, the pain has increased sharply and my vision has started to blur. My new eyes are the work of magic. They can't function normally here. As much as I despise the universe of the Demonata, I'm a slave of it now.

As I'm working on the window, I hear the whispers from the mysterious small lights. I glance around and spot several pulsing rapidly. But the whispers don't seem to be directed at me this time. And they're not repeating a single word. There's a steady stream of phrases, none of which I can make sense of.

Behind me, Dervish and Beranabus are arguing. Dervish wants to stay and find out more about the werewolves. Beranabus says we can't waste time on them. Meera sides with Dervish. There have been lots of crossings recently and the Disciples are struggling to cope. She's afraid the werewolves might be used to target members of the secret group. If they killed a large number of the mages, demons could cross freely.

Even though I'm not paying a huge amount of attention to the argument, I find myself pausing. "It might be related," I say.

"Related to what?" Bec asks. Beranabus waves her silent and frowns at me.

"This could be part of the Shadow's plan," I tell him, the words tumbling out by themselves. The whispers from the lights have increased. I have to concentrate hard to drown them out. "It could be trying to create scores of windows so that its army of demons can break through at once. We'll need the Disciples if that's the case — we can't be everywhere at the same time to stop them all."

"Maybe," Beranabus says. "But that doesn't alter the fact that Dervish will last about five minutes if we leave him here."

"I'll be fine," Dervish snarls.

"No," Beranabus says. "Your heart is finished. You'll die within days. That's not a guess," he adds before Dervish can argue. "And you wouldn't be able to do much during that time, apart from wheeze and clutch your chest a lot."

"It's really that bad?" Dervish asks quietly.

Beranabus nods. "In the universe of magic, you might survive. Here, you're a dead man walking."

"Then get him there quick," Grubbs says. "I'll stay."

"Not you too," Beranabus groans. "What did I do to deserve as stubborn and reckless a pair as you?"

"It makes sense," Grubbs insists. "If the attacks were Lord Loss looking to get even, they're irrelevant. But if they're related to the Shadow, we need to know. I can confront the Lambs, find out if they're mixed up with the demon master, stop them if they are."

"Is the Shadow the creature we saw in the cave?" Bec asks.

"Aye," Beranabus says. "We haven't learnt much about it, except that it's put together an army of demons and is working hard to launch them across to our world."

He stares at Grubbs, and as he pauses, the whispers change. They're softer now, almost musical. I feel uneasy, even slightly sick, but I've no idea why.

"You'd operate alone?" Beranabus asks.

"I'd need help," Grubbs replies, and asks for Shark and Meera's assistance. While they discuss that, I focus on the window again. I'm close to opening it. The whispers of the lights have almost died away. I feel worse than ever, as if we're in great danger. But there's no reason to be afraid... is there?

A pale green window opens. Beranabus still hasn't chosen whether or not to let Grubbs stay. "Time to decide," I tell him, and as I say that, the whispers spark up again.

"Very well," Beranabus snaps at Grubbs. "But listen to Shark and Meera, heed their advice and contact me before you go running up against the likes of Lord Loss or the Shadow." He picks up the unconscious Sharmila. "Follow me, Bec," he says and steps through the window.

Bec doesn't leave immediately. She's confused, not sure of what's happening. Dervish is busy saying goodbye to Grubbs and Meera, wishing them luck, cursing the fact that he can't stay and help them. As he finally stumbles through the window, Grubbs has a short chat with Bec. Then she faces me. She looks more lost than I feel. As difficult as it is, I force a smile. "The world moves quickly when Beranabus is around," I tell her, trying to cheer her up.

"What's it like through there?" she asks, staring at the window with quiet terror.

"Bad." My smile slips. "The Shadow's promising the eradication of mankind and a new dawn of demon rule. Others have threatened that before, but it's convinced an army of demons – even powerful masters like Lord Loss – that it can make good on its vow. We could be looking at the end this time." I take a step into the window of light but don't cross fully, straddling two universes at the same time. I wave Bec forward. "Let's go."

She looks back once, then follows me through the

window to an oasis in the demon universe which Beranabus and I are familiar with. We'll be safe here, for a while at least.

But I take no comfort from our security. I'm steady on my feet, maintaining a calm front, but inside my head sirens are blaring, my thoughts a million miles removed from werewolves, the Lambs, Juni Swan and the Shadow. I feel sicker than when I saw the dismembered babies in the hospital.

I've realised why the whispers unnerved me. That final burst of chattering, just before Beranabus made his decision to let Grubbs go, clued me in to what was really happening.

Beranabus should have brought Grubbs along. He's been wary of uniting the pieces of the Kah-Gash, but this was the time to risk it. Our enemies are on the move, trying to kill one of us or get their hands on a piece of the ancient weapon. Beranabus should have kept us all with him, if not to unleash the power of the Kah-Gash, then to protect us. We'd be a lot safer if we stuck together. Leaving Grubbs behind was madness.

Why did someone as experienced as Beranabus make such a slip? And why did the others – myself included – go along with his bad call?

Answer — the lights. The whispers influenced us. Something didn't want us to band together, so it subtly interfered and split us up, making it seem as if it was our own choice. We're being manipulated by the whispers of the lights!

# LYING LOW

→I can't tell the others about the lights, the whispers or my suspicion that we are being used. I want to, but whenever I try to share my fears, my lips seize up. I'm unable to speak, or else everyday rubbish spills out and we end up talking about something else. I've tried writing, scribbling a warning in the sand of the oasis, but my fingers clench and turn against me.

When we first stepped through the window, I thought I might have imagined the whispers or the influence they're exerting over us. Now I'm sure I called it right. The lights did – *do* – control us. They must have planted a hidden command inside my brain that makes me clam up whenever I try to share my misgivings.

While I struggle to break through the spell, the others argue about what to do next. Beranabus wants to hunt the Shadow, pick up where we left off. Dervish is against that. He's determined to go after Juni, to settle old scores.

I stay out of the arguments for a couple of days. But when Dervish is pressing his claim for the umpteenth time, trying to sway Beranabus by saying we might be able to torture Juni to find out information about the Shadow, the small, ever-changing lights pulse and the air hums with whispers only I can hear.

"We can't go after Lord Loss directly — he's too powerful," I find myself telling Beranabus, and although I know these aren't my words, that I'm being used like a puppet, I can't stop. "But we can target Juni. Lord Loss didn't show himself at the hospital, but Juni was acting on his behalf. She might have been part of the group in Carcery Vale too. If more assaults on the Disciples are planned, she'll possibly act as the go-between again, conveying Lord Loss's orders to their allies. If we can trap her, we can find out what she knows about the Shadow."

Beranabus thinks that makes sense – or the lights make him think it – so he tells me to focus on Juni, track her movements and let him know when she slips out of Lord Loss's realm.

I want to scream foul and tell them we're being toyed with, but my lips gum up. I throw everything I have at the spell, to no avail. In the end I do as Beranabus bids. I retire to one of the fake trees – the oasis is dotted with trees made of bones and scraps of flesh – and sit in the shade, glumly training my thoughts on Juni Swan.

→As days pass, the others recuperate. Beranabus and Bec fashioned new legs for Sharmila out of the bones and skin of the trees when we arrived, and she adapts to them smoothly. Bec has worked a lot with Dervish, drawing on her healing powers, doing what she can for his faltering heart. Neither he nor Sharmila can live on Earth again, but as long as they stay in this universe of magic they can function almost normally.

The four of them pass a lot of the time duelling, sharpening their reflexes, testing their skills. Magic is all about trial and error. Even after thousands of years, Beranabus is still discovering new aspects of himself, depending on what's thrown at him.

I'd like to join them, but I've been given a task and Beranabus doesn't take it kindly when one of his assistants disobeys a direct order. So I keep to myself, studying the lights and focusing on Juni Swan and her master.

It's difficult because of the whispers. The murmurs come regularly while I'm concentrating, not as strongly as at the hospital, but distracting none the less. I can't stop thinking about the spell they've woven. Is it the work of the Shadow? Unlikely — if the creature could exert such influence, it would turn us against one another.

The Kah-Gash? A weapon that can destroy universes and distort the laws of time would have no difficulty bending a few humans to its will. But the Kah-Gash would surely have wanted me, Grubbs and Bec together, to unite so it could be reassembled.

If not the Shadow or the Kah-Gash, who can be controlling the lights? Are they self-conscious, some new life form? Or maybe I'm imagining them. I've doubted my sanity in the past. Maybe this time I've cracked for real.

Finally, after a week of self-torment and doubt, I sense Juni opening a window and leaving Lord Loss's world.

"She's moving," I tell the others, disrupting their latest duel.

They crowd around me. "Where did she go?" Beranabus asks.

"Earth," I say after a brief pause to confirm her location.

"And Lord Loss?"

"He stayed in his own realm."

"Can you tell where she is exactly?" Dervish asks.

"No. I should be able to, but I can't place it." That worries me more than I reveal.

"Is she close to Grubbs?" Dervish presses.

I do a quick scan and shake my head.

"Well?" Sharmila asks Beranabus.

"Kernel and I will investigate," he says. "The rest of you stay here."

"Nuts to that," Dervish huffs.

"Don't forget about your heart," Beranabus says. "Or Sharmila's legs. You're a pair of wrecks on that world. Let us check the situation and report back. We won't engage her if we can avoid it."

"What about me?" Bec asks. "I can survive there."

"Aye, but I'm asking you to wait. Please. Until we know more about what we're walking into."

I'd like to know more about it too before I cross. But I've lived with Beranabus long enough to know he doesn't hold much faith in the philosophy of look-before-you-leap. Except for his edgy pursuit of the Shadow, I've never seen him act cautiously. He believes it's best to jump in the fire and deal with the flames when they're licking the soles of your feet.

Keeping silent about my fears, I slot patches of light together and open a white window. With my back to the others, I offer up a quick prayer, the kind I used to reel off when I was a fresh apprentice, before I grew hardened to the terrors of the Demonata. Then, sensing Beranabus behind me, I step forward into the unknown.

# DEATH WATCH

→We find ourselves on the deck of a massive ship, close to a swimming pool. Deckchairs are strewn about the place. Bodies everywhere, ripped to pieces, stomachs carved open, heads and limbs torn loose. Puddles of blood merge and spread slowly, seeping into the cracks between the planks. The water of the swimming pool is a deep, dead red.

Beranabus ignores the corpses. He's seen worse in his time. I have too. But it still hits me hard whenever I walk into a nightmarish scene like this. It only takes me a few seconds to recover, but Beranabus doesn't even need that. He's instantly alert, looking for threats, sizing up the situation. I see him relax slightly and, once I overcome my initial shock, I realise why. The area is charged with magic. We're on Earth, but it feels like the Demonata's universe. We can operate at full capacity here.

"We're encased," Beranabus says. "The ship's been sealed off by a bubble of magic. They must have a lodestone."

Lodestones are rocks which were filled with magic by beings known as the Old Creatures. They ruled our world in the distant past, holding the demons at bay. They fled many generations ago, but left the charged stones behind. Many have drained of power over the centuries, and Beranabus destroyed most of the others, to stop the Demonata's power-hungry mages from making use of them. But some remain, secreted away, either unknown to him, inaccessible or indestructible. Demons or evil mages sometimes find them and use them to open limited tunnels between universes, allowing the Demonata to spend more time here and wreak maximum havoc.

"Where's Juni?" Beranabus asks.

"Lower down. I thought it would be wiser not to face her until we'd assessed the risk. I don't know if anyone's with her, but there's an open window. It's not very sturdy. Only weak demons could cross through it."

Beranabus thinks about that, then says, "I'm going back for the others." He steps through the window, leaving me with the dead.

The silence is disturbing. I play out crazy scenarios inside my head, imagining the corpses coming back to life and attacking. I've never seen a zombie film. I heard about *Night of the Living Dead* when I was a child, but my parents wouldn't let me watch it.

I don't have any hair – I've always been bald – but if I did, it would be standing on end. I've got a bad case of what my mother used to call the heebie-jeebies. I want to duck through the window after Beranabus. This ship is bad news. We'll wind up dead if we stay, bleeding sacks of flesh and bone.

Before I can bolt, Beranabus returns and the others cross after him. My nerves settle and I laugh away my fears. Zombies — ridiculous! I've seen enough of the universe to know we need never fear the dead, only the living.

The Disciples are nervous. Bec scans the lower decks and says there's only one demon on board with Juni. I tell the others about the open window.

"We should go back," Sharmila says. "Juni has set this up to ensnare us."

"Why would she be expecting us?" Dervish asks.

"Lord Loss may have reasoned that we would target Juni. Perhaps everything – the attacks on Dervish, Juni revealing herself on the roof of the hospital – was designed to lure Beranabus here. The demon master might be poised to cross and finish us off personally."

"Not through that window," I tell Sharmila, certain no demon master could make use of the opening close to Juni.

"Then through another," she says. "We have never been able to explain why Lord Loss can cross when other masters cannot, or how he goes about it."

Beranabus sighs. "You could be right, but we might never get a better shot at Juni. If she's not expecting us, it's the perfect time to strike. If she is and this is a trap, at least we can anticipate the worst. The magic in the air means she'll be dangerous, but it serves us as much as her. If Lord Loss doesn't turn up, we can match her. If he does cross, we'll make a swift getaway."

"Are you sure of that?" Sharmila frowns. "If we have to open a new window…"

"We won't," Beranabus says. "Kernel will stay here and guard our escape route. You'll know if any other windows open, won't you?"

"Yes," I say confidently.

"Then keep this one alive and watch for signs of further activity. If you sense anything, summon us and we'll withdraw. Is everyone satisfied with that?"

Sharmila is still dubious, but she shrugs. I'm not happy either. I don't want to stay by myself, surrounded by corpses. But we need to protect our only way out. Besides, I'll be safer up here than down there. Beranabus is doing me a favour, though I'm sure he's thinking only of his own well-being, not mine.

As they make their way across the deck, I move closer to the window and pat a couple of patches back into place. Windows never remain stable for more than a few minutes, but I have the power to keep them open indefinitely. If demons were able to manipulate the lights like I can, mankind would have been wiped out long ago.

The minutes pass with agonising slowness. The sun is relentless and my mouth is dry. I could easily find something to drink, but I don't want to abandon my post. I'm sure I could open another window if this one blinks out of existence but I don't want to take any chances. I'm not sure how lodestones work. Maybe Juni could use its power to slow me down.

As I'm concentrating, trying not to obsess about the mounds of corpses around me, the smaller, unpredictable patches of light begin to pulse. "Not now," I groan, but the patches ignore me. Moments later come the whispers. Faster, more urgently than before. I tense, expecting to find myself acting against my wishes. Maybe they'll make me close the window or head after the others, to die with them in the ship's hold.

But nothing happens. If the lights are trying to influence me, they're failing. Ignoring them, I focus on the window, holding it in place, keeping the shape.

Something flickers to my left. I turn and see a

group of the small patches click together. They swirl over and around one another, a mini vortex of various hues and shades of light.

More patches are attracted to the cluster. It grows and spins faster, changing shape, pulsing rapidly. The whispers grow louder, become shouts. I don't know what's happening, but it can only be bad news. I wish the others were here, so we could abandon this place immediately.

When almost all of the small lights have joined and are whirling around, they suddenly zip towards me. Yelping, I throw myself aside. I expect them to chase me, but then I see that I was never their target. They were aiming for the window. They slap into it and shimmer across the face of the white panel. As I sit up and stare, the window becomes a multicoloured rip in the air.

The whispers die away. Silence falls. I stand but don't approach the window. I study it cautiously, fearfully. The lights pulse rapidly, then slide towards the centre, all the colours angling to the focal point, drawn to it as if by gravity.

Then — an explosion. A ball of light bursts from the heart of the window and shoots across the ship's swimming pool, circling it in a spiral pattern, like a punctured balloon careening across a room. The window resumes its white colour.

The ball circles the pool a few more times, then drifts towards the deck and comes to a halt three or four feet above it. The ball is rainbow-coloured, about the size of a large dog, though its shape changes constantly. It reminds me of the jellyish substance in a lava lamp, the way it oozes from one form into another, altering all the time.

"What the hell are you?" I gasp, not expecting an answer. But to my astonishment I receive one.

"I have no name."

I've seen a lot of crazy stuff over the last few years that would leave most people's jaws hanging. I thought I was immune to surprise. But this blows me away. All I can do is gawp at the ball of light like a five-year-old who's walked in on Santa Claus.

"You must come with me," the voice says. I don't know where the words are coming from. They seem to be forming inside my head.

"*Come...*" the voice insists.

"Come where?" I croak. "Who are you? *What* are you?"

"There will be time for explanations later. We must depart this world before..." The voice stops and there's a sighing sound. "Too late."

"What do you mean?"

Before the ball of light can answer, my crazy fantasy of a few minutes ago becomes a reality. All around me, the corpses on the deck shudder, twitch, then clamber to their feet. As impossible as it is, the dead have come back to life, and they're focusing their glinting, hungry eyes on *me*.

# COME...

→The rising dead terrify me more than any demon ever did. Demons are natural. They obey certain laws. You know what to expect when you face one of them. But the dead aren't supposed to return. When a body perishes, the soul moves on. That's the way it's always been. But someone must have forgotten to mention that to these walking, snarling, slavering corpses.

I stand like a simpleton, watching them advance. I'd heard that zombies in movies walk slowly, stiffly, mechanically. Not these. They don't have the look of living people, but they move like them, fluidly and firmly.

As the dead close in on me, teeth exposed, hands outstretched, the ball of light flits over their heads and flares, causing them to cover their eyes and stumble to a halt. They mewl like newborn calves and lash out at the light.

"*Come...*" the voice repeats. "Cross while they are distracted."

"Where?" I howl, gaze fixed on the zombies.

"*Come...*" is the only response. The ball of light skims over the heads of the walking dead and hovers by the window.

"I can't," I whisper, studying the ranks of animated corpses. "The others..."

"Doomed," the voice says. "You cannot worry about them. They are no longer your concern. *Come...*" It sounds impatient.

A man without a chest – it's been ripped away, exposing the bones of his spine and shoulders – lowers his arms and blinks. Realising he can see again, he sets his sights on me and rushes forward, howling wildly.

My hands, which have been trembling by my sides, shoot up and I unleash a ball of energy. The dead man flies backwards, knocking down those behind him. As others converge, I blast them with magic and back up close to the window.

"Yes," the voice murmurs approvingly.

But I've no intention of going anywhere with this freakish ball of talking light. I ran out on Beranabus once, long ago. Never again.

Taking a firm stand, I construct an invisible barrier, a circle of magic six or seven feet in diameter, through which the dead can't pass. I'm not good at this type of magic. I doubt I could put a barrier in place strong enough to stop a demon. But if these revived corpses are only as strong as they were in life, it should repel them.

My stomach rumbles with fear as the zombies cluster around the barrier. They scrape, punch, kick and spit at it. I hear – imagine – a creaking noise. I reinforce the barrier, sweating desperately, and turn 360 degrees, trying to cover every angle at once, ensuring there are no weak points.

There aren't. The barrier holds. As long as the magic in the air remains, I can keep these wretched zombies at bay.

I've been holding my breath. Letting it out, I bend over and smile raggedly. I even manage a weak laugh. That would have been an awful death. To stand up to one powerful demon after another, only to fall to a pack of alarming but relatively weak zombies... It would have been a shameful way to go.

"You have done well," the voice says, pulsing eagerly by the window. "Now come with me. We must leave this world. We have far to go."

I straighten and study the ball of light. I'm glad of the excuse not to look at the writhing zombies, especially the children, every bit as ravenous as the adults.

"I'm going nowhere without the others," I tell it.

"They do not matter. You are the one we need. *Come...*"

"Who are 'we'?" I challenge the voice. "What do you want? Where–"

The ship lurches. I'm thrown sideways, towards the ranks of living dead. I yell with shock, but the barrier deflects me away from the gnashing, grabbing zombies.

I get to my feet slowly, rubbing my arm where I collided with the barrier. The ship has tilted. The water in the swimming pool is starting to spill out over the lowest edge, and some of the deckchairs are sliding backwards. A few of the zombies slip away from the barrier, but they're back again moments later.

"What's happening?" I ask the ball of light.

"The ship is sinking," it answers. "Beranabus has been killed. Come now, before it is too late."

It takes a few seconds for that to hit. At first I'm just panicked that the ship's going down. Then the full impact of the statement rams home. "*Beranabus?*" I gasp.

"The Shadow killed him."

"No!" I shake my head wildly. Beranabus can't be dead. The world doesn't make sense without him. He's single-handedly held back the hordes of demons for more than a thousand years. I knew he was old and tired, and he often spoke half-heartedly of retiring. But secretly I believed he was invincible, that he'd live forever, reborn like a phoenix when he grew tired of the confines of his old bones.

"There will be no rebirth," the voice says calmly as everything collapses into chaos. "Beranabus is dead. This world will have to struggle on without him. You must come with me. You *must*."

I expect tears, but there aren't any. I'm devastated by the loss of Beranabus, and maybe I'll weep for him later, but for now I'm dry-eyed. When I'm sure I'm not going to cry, I look at the light again. This time I regard it with a hint of loathing.

"You set this up," I snarl. "You led us here. You're in league with Juni Swan."

"No," the voice says. "We do not serve the Demonata."

"You split us from Grubbs," I accuse it. "You forced me to advise Beranabus to focus on Juni. This is your work as much as it's hers."

The ball is silent for a moment. "You were aware of our guiding hand," it says. "Interesting. You see and hear more than we thought."

"Yes." I laugh roughly. "And I see through you now. Beranabus would be alive if we hadn't come here. You manipulated us."

"To an extent," the voice agrees. "We needed a lodestone. I could not make the final push to your world without one. So we influenced you and your foes, and tempted you to this place. It is unfortunate that it resulted in Beranabus's death, but that is an acceptable loss. All that matters is that you come with me. Everything else is immaterial."

"Bull!" I snort.

The ball of light flickers. "I do not understand."

"I'm going nowhere. My friends are here — Bec, Dervish, Sharmila. I'm staying to help them. I promised I'd keep this window open and I will."

"No," the voice says. "We cannot wait. If you fall, all is lost. I do not have the power to reclaim your fragment of the Kah-Gash. It would go to–"

"So that's it!" I yell. "You want the weapon."

"Only your part."

"You can't have it," I sneer, taking a step away from the window.

The ball turns dark blue, before resuming its normal variety of colours. I think it just lost its temper.

"You cannot defy us," the voice says. "You must come with me. It is vital."

I shake my head and back up to within a couple of inches of the barrier. "My friends come first. Always."

The ball pulses for a few seconds. Then the voice says, "Very well."

The light flicks up over my head and cuts through the barrier, vanishing into the crowd of zombies. The deck is rising steadily. The pool is almost empty now. Some of the less sturdy zombies have started to slide down the deck, towards the end dipping into the sea. But most remain pinned to the barrier.

More worrying than the zombies or the disappearance of the ball of light is the fading magic. The bubble around the ship is intact, but the magical energy is dwindling. I can still maintain the barrier, but not for long.

I think about retreating, closing the window behind me, then building a new one, opening it to whatever level of the ship Grubbs and the others are on. It wouldn't take more than a few minutes. But they might not have even that short time. If they make it to the upper deck, this window offers their fastest route out. If I disable it, they'll have to wait, besieged by zombies, and that might be asking too much of them. Better to linger as long as I can, and only resort to the other plan if the barrier cracks.

As I make up my mind to stay, a man steps through the crowd. Most of his throat has been chewed away. His head's attached to his torso by stray strands of flesh and muscle. He puts his hands on the barrier, palms flat. His calm expression is in sharp contrast to the twisted grimaces of the other zombies. As I stare at the man, wondering why he looks different, light flickers in his eyes. I realise that the ball of light has wormed its way into the zombie and possessed him. Before I can do anything, the man steps through the barrier and clutches me.

"Do not fight," he gurgles, pushing me towards the window.

"Let go!" I roar, wrestling wildly. I manage to slip loose. I think about darting through the window, but that's where the light wants me to go. Before I can come up with an alternate plan, the zombie grabs me again.

"We do not want to hurt you," he says, nudging me closer to the window of white light. "You must trust us. We only want–"

I knee the man in the stomach. Even though he's dead, he winces with pain or the memory of it.

As I prepare to break free, I spot Bec, Sharmila, Dervish and a man I don't recognise. They're fighting against the tilt of the ship, forcing their way towards me, battling through zombies. Bec spots me locked in combat.

"Kernel!" she shouts. "Hold on. We're almost with you. We–"

"The lights!" I roar back in reply. "The lights are doing this! Don't–"

"Enough," the man snaps. "You are coming. *Now.*"

I reach for his head, to tear it all the way off. Before I can, the man's eyes open wide and the ball of light gushes from them, as well as from his mouth and the gap in his throat. The light is blinding. I squeeze my eyelids shut, but the glare sears through them and I see almost as clearly as if they were open.

As light streams from the man, he explodes, his body ripping apart as if someone had planted a stick of dynamite inside him. The blast sends me flying backwards, through the window, which shatters behind me, stranding the others and cutting me off from the world of all things human.

# TRIPPING THE LIGHT FANTASTIC

→The ball of light sails through the window with me. It completely envelops me, crackling over my creamy brown skin, tickling my hairless scalp, buzzing in my ears. I'm warm and comfortable in its embrace. I think this is what it must be like for a baby in its mother's womb.

I try to fight the enveloping light, to break free of its hold, but it just buckles and bulges to match my movements. Finally I settle back and conserve my energy, saving it for when I can focus it more usefully.

I study my surroundings. Though the multicoloured ball of light holds me in its grasp like fingers clutched around a coin, it's translucent. There are other lights beyond, patches and panels, a dazzling variety of colours and sizes. They fill the area around us completely. No stars, sky or planets. A universe of lights.

We're floating through them, sliding from one patch to another, following some sort of hidden path. I hope. Or maybe there's no path and we're lost. Perhaps this is what the lights wanted all along, to strand me in this wilderness. But I don't think so. We seem to be moving meaningfully. Or is that just wishful thinking?

Whatever the truth, I've never experienced anything like this before. Whenever I've stepped through a window, I've emerged instantly on another world. This is like travelling through an immense tunnel.

"Correct," the voice says. The ball of light can evidently read my thoughts, which is bad news — I can't spring any surprises. "We are travelling further than you have ever been, but we are still in your universe. Space is not as easily traversed here as in the Demonata's realm."

"Where are we going?" I ask. Except I don't ask out loud. My mouth won't open. "What's going on?" I cry silently.

"There is no oxygen," the voice explains. "You are cocooned. It is the easiest way to travel. Don't worry — it will not last long and you won't be harmed."

I'm not sure I trust the voice, but there's nothing I can do except lie back and accept it. "So where are we going?" I ask again, trying to sound casual.

"You will find out soon," the voice replies and says nothing more, leaving me to study the spectacular light show in awed, helpless silence.

→After several minutes we zone in on a massive patch of green light. As we pass through, the cocoon around me slips away and I tumble to a cracked stone floor. My mouth opens and I drag in a lungful of acidic but breathable air. Pinching my nose shut to block out the stench, I look around. I'm in a domed chamber. The ball of light hangs in the air several feet away, pulsing steadily. The stones around us are throbbing in unison.

Blanking my thoughts, desperate not to betray myself, I back away. There's an exit behind me. As I reach it, I pause, expecting the ball of light to shoot across and block my way. When nothing happens, I slip out of the chamber and scurry through a short, narrow tunnel.

The tunnel opens out on to a plateau. I race away from the chamber, planning to put plenty of space between myself and the ball of light. But the air here is foul and my body revolts. As a stitch hits me hard, I collapse, gasping for air, lungs straining, head aching.

After a minute of painful gasping, the stitch eases and I stand. Instead of running again, I turn slowly and study my surroundings. I'm on a ruined world. The sky is a dark purple colour, full of poisonous-looking clouds. Forks of lightning split the air every few seconds although I can hear no thunder. When the lightning hits the ground, the dark earth flashes and explodes in short-lived funnels of dirt, mud and pebbles.

Huge, bone like pillars jut out of the scorched, pockmarked earth. At first I think they're the remains of giant demons. I've seen plenty of sky demons in my time, massive monsters, some the size of a world. But the longer I look, the more convinced I become that these aren't bones, but rather the remains of buildings.

Wandering slowly to the nearest pile of pillars, breathing shallowly, I find that they're made of some sort of metal. That confuses me. Demons aren't builders. Some create houses or palaces, even towns and cities, modelled after those on Earth. But they use bones, flesh, cobwebs, plants and other organic substances to fashion their facsimiles. I've never known a demon to utilise metal or concrete.

The voice told me we were still in the human universe. I thought we slipped out of it when we crossed through the window, but it looks like we didn't. I don't know where I am, but I'm pretty sure it's not a demon world.

As I move through the ash-ridden remains of what was once maybe a skyscraper, something moves in the filth nearby. Jumping backwards, I try to absorb magic from the air, but there's virtually nothing to tap into. Like Earth, this is a zone of little or no magical energy.

The thing wriggles clear of the hard mud and debris it was nestling beneath. It looks like a giant slug, but with six small eyes, a jagged gash for a mouth, and other human-looking bits and pieces — a few fingers, a toe, a strip of flesh that might be an ear. The eyes stare at me for a moment, then the mouth opens and it thrusts itself at my face, making a gruesome, high-pitched noise.

The slug creature strikes my chest and I fall. It's on me in a flash, slithering to my face, leaving a slimy trail. Thin fingers scratch at my chin, then a grey, cold slit clamps over my mouth and nostrils. I feel it tighten on my lips and nose, and the slug squeals with excitement as I struggle for air.

I punch the slug, but my fists make little impact, merely sinking into the gooey, sticky layers of its body. Disgusting slime oozes from the slit, filling my mouth. I collapse, my lungs straining, still pushing and punching the slug, but feebly now. My strength is fading. Soon I'll be slug fodder and the beast will be able to feast on my flesh at its leisure.

As the world starts to darken around me, the slug is abruptly ripped away. I catch a glimpse of it flying through the air, squealing frantically. It lands hard, rolls a few times, then straightens and propels itself at me again.

Somebody steps in front of me and meets the charge of the slug. It looks like a boy, but with pale green skin. He's small but strong — he catches the slug and slams it down in a neatly executed wrestling move. While the slug writhes beneath him, the boy grabs one of the creature's fingers and bites it off with… a small mouth set in the palm of his hand!

The slug stunned me when it attacked, but when I realise who the boy is I'm shocked to the core. I stare with mounting horror and bewilderment as the slug shrieks, then quickly slips away when the boy releases it. He makes sure it isn't going to attack again, then turns to face me.

He has the body of a young child – maybe three years old – but a head that's bigger than an adult's. Mouths in both palms, full of small, sharp teeth. No eyes — instead, balls of fire burn deeply in his empty sockets. And no hair — in its place, small slugs, much like the one he just saved me from, slide slowly around his skull.

"*Artery!*" I moan. I have no idea how Lord Loss's familiar came to be here – he was killed a year ago – but I'm certain he only saved me from the slug in order to kill me himself.

The hellchild cocks his head and frowns. "No," he

growls, and it's the first time I've ever heard him speak. His green flesh ripples and the colour fades. His head shrinks and the slugs burrow into his scalp, then turn into hair. The fire in his empty sockets dies away and eyes sprout to fill them. His large mouth tightens a couple of notches and his sharp teeth soften into a more human-like shape. The mouths in his palms disappear, flesh closing over them.

"No," he says again, and this time his voice is softer. "Not Artery." He glances at his skin – pale, like Mum's – and smiles. Almost no trace of the monster remains. I'm gazing at what looks like an ordinary boy. And he's every bit as familiar as the green-skinned demon.

"I'm *Art*," he says, then steps forward and sticks out a small, delicate hand.

# THE MAN FROM ATLANTIS

→"You can't be real," I gasp, backing away from the figure. "You're not my brother. You never really existed. I made you up."

"Yes," the boy nods. "You transformed Artery into this shape and kept him safe, even though he should have perished on your world, by subconsciously utilising the power of the Kah-Gash. We were surprised it cooperated with you. But the Kah-Gash never ceases to surprise us."

"You're not Art!" I shout. "Art didn't speak like this. He never spoke at all."

"True," the boy says. "Artery could communicate with his own kind, but only telepathically. Art would never have been able to speak, even if he'd grown up.

"I'm not the demon you stole or the child you turned it into," the boy continues. "I am the ball of light from the ship. Sensing the difficulty you had accepting my natural form, I adopted the body of someone you would feel more comfortable with. If you prefer, I can switch to the shape of your mother or father, but I think you will find me easier to deal with this way."

My head's spinning. "Are you a shape-shifter?" I ask, getting to my feet and walking around the boy, checking him from every angle.

"No," he says. "I have no physical body. I assembled this from a corpse, remoulding its flesh and bones. It was a creature like the one which attacked you. They are pitiful beasts. Hard to believe they are descended from beings once as industrious as yourself."

"What do you mean?" I frown.

"It's a descendant of the Atlanteans," Art says. "They were bipeds, like you, and their society was similar to yours. Indeed, your distant ancestors were strongly influenced by the beings of Atlantis."

"*Atlantis?*" I croak. "What are you talking about? Atlantis was a mythical city."

"No," Art corrects me. "It was a world of immense, amazing cities, the closest inhabitable planet to Earth. The Atlanteans explored this world to its fullest, then the lifeless planets nearby, finally extending to their neighbouring galaxies. They visited your world. Your ancestors worshipped them, built monuments like theirs, dressed in their honour, wrote things down as they did."

"Are you pulling my leg?" I growl.

"I do not understand," Art responds.

"Are you trying to fool me?"

"No. Atlantis was an advanced planet. The Atlanteans were wise and kind. But they harnessed the raw energy of this universe and that is dangerous. They knew the risks and accepted them. It was the price they paid to explore further afield, beyond the confines of their own sector of the universe.

"They fell within the space of an hour," Art goes on, and although he has a child's face, he looks like an adult as he gazes upon the wrecks of the buildings. "An explosion set off a chain reaction and their society crumbled. The ships they'd sent off into space were linked to the home world, so they were destroyed too. The sky filled with pollutants and ash. Death claimed nineteen billion souls. A few Atlanteans survived and mutated, but I doubt they would have wished for their offspring to end up like this. It would have been better if they'd all perished."

Art falls silent. I stare at the boy who is the image of the child I once thought of as a brother. Now that I'm over my initial shock, I find that he was right — it's a lot easier talking to someone who looks like a boy than with a ball of light.

I study the graveyard of the world around me. Art could be lying, but I don't think so. I'm standing on the remains of Atlantis. The most famous lost city of legend was never a city at all, but a different world. The information is mind-boggling. If Art's telling the truth, the Atlanteans visited mankind in the past. They taught us to read and write, to build. Maybe they even bred with us and–

"No," Art interrupts. "The Atlanteans did not breed with lesser beings."

"This is incredible," I gasp, the word not doing my feelings justice. "But if they travelled to our world by rockets, not windows, is this still the human universe?"

"Of course." Art sounds surprised. "I thought that was clear."

"You said we hadn't crossed but I wasn't sure."

"We have not left your universe and will not during the course of our travels," Art says.

"This isn't the end?"

The boy giggles the way Art used to when he bit someone. "Hardly. This is merely the beginning of an amazing journey."

"Where are we going?" I ask.

"Far away," he answers mysteriously.

"What if I don't want to go with you?" I counter.

"You have no choice," Art says.

"Is that a threat?"

"No," he shrugs. "It's just the way things are."

"Who – or what – the hell are you?" I snap.

"Those who know us give us many names," Art says. "Your people called us the Old Creatures."

"Beranabus told me about them. He..." That reminds me of the ancient mage's death and the danger the others face. "We have to go back!" I cry. "You've got to take me home, so I can–"

"That won't happen," Art says firmly. "Purge yourself of the notion. We have come far from your world. As skilled as you are at manipulating the strings of the universe, you cannot find your way back alone. You must see this journey through to its end."

"What sort of an end?" I hiss. "Where are you taking me? And if you're not specific this time, forget it — I'm not going to wander aimlessly through the universe with you. I'd rather stay here with the slugs."

"Very well," Art says. "We are travelling to the birthplace of all things, where time and space began. We call it the Crux. And it lies at the centre of both this universe and the Demonata's."

"That doesn't make sense," I complain.

"Don't worry," Art smiles smugly. "By the end it will."

# UNDER THE SEA

→I try thinking of a way to outwit the Old Creature. While I might not be able to open a window back to Earth, I'm sure I can open one to the demon universe and return home from there. But Art reads my mind and chuckles.

"I will not permit it."

"You can't stop me," I retort.

"Actually I can. I have the power to tear apart any window that you create, and I can do it before the window opens. If necessary, we can stay here for decades and duel with one another, but I would not recommend it. You would lose."

I start work on a window, to test him, but Art's smug expression stops me. He's telling the truth. Cursing, I begin to question him again, but he only turns and walks back to the stone chamber, where a dark grey window is waiting for us.

"What is it to be?" Art asks.

Since I've no real choice, I snarl and step forward with him.

Just before I reach the window, Art's body unravels and he becomes a ball of multicoloured light again. "I have to travel like this," he tells me, his words sounding inside my head. "I need to cocoon you again. But I will resume the shape of Art when we come to our next stop."

"Whatever," I sniff unhappily, bitter at being manipulated.

The light sweeps over and surrounds me. When Art gives the command, I step into the window and we progress.

→Over the next few hours we pass through several chambers similar to the one on Atlantis. Some are made of stone, but others are carved out of wood, metal or other substances. One is simply a chamber of lights, a dome of panels and patches. We don't leave any of these chambers, just stay long enough for Art to open a new window, then move on again.

I'm still amazed by Atlantis, stunned by the proof of other life forms in our universe. I always assumed we weren't alone, that there were intelligent beings on other worlds. But to see an actual alien was an incredible experience. Even if it did just look like a big slug!

Art's a quiet guide. He concentrates on steering us from one chamber to the next. I don't think it's easy.

These patches of lights aren't as easily mastered as the ones I'm accustomed to. It seems to be hard work.

I'm still worried about Dervish and the others, and in shock about the loss of Beranabus. But there's nothing I can do, so I lie back and bide my time. I'm in the grip of something more powerful than myself. I don't understand it and I can't fight or escape. *Yet*.

→We pass through another window and I find myself in a water-logged chamber. I'm not sure what the walls are made of, but it looks like seaweed. As we slip through, parts of the walls glow. It's not magic — I can see small organisms in the crevices of the greenish blocks. They're like underwater glow-worms.

"We will rest a while," Art says, letting the window close behind us. The lights surrounding me shimmer, then slip off, although a layer remains, keeping me dry and providing me with air.

"That's clever," I note as the ball of light transforms into a boy.

"What?" Art frowns.

"The shield."

"It is nothing special."

"Are you tired?" I ask, detecting weariness in his tone.

"Yes." He sighs. "Travel of this nature is draining. We

don't normally cross vast distances so swiftly. But time is against us, so I must push myself."

"How far have we come?"

He pauses, then says, "You do not have words to describe it. Your scientists do, but their terms would mean nothing to you."

Art heads towards a gap in the glowing blocks and I glide after him. We exit the chamber and I'm confronted with an underwater paradise. I'm blown away by what I see and it takes a minute before I can do anything except bob up and down in the water and stare.

We're in the middle of a city. The buildings are all kinds of weird shapes, made of seaweed, shells and huge, twisting roots. Many rise far above and deep below us, two hundred floors high, maybe more. Most sway gently. All sorts of colours, illuminated by enormous swathes of the glowing organisms I saw in the chamber.

There are no roads, just avenues between, through and around the buildings. No glass or doors, only scores of holes in the structures.

I spot some creatures. There are hordes – schools? – of them all around us, floating along the avenues, darting in and out of holes in the buildings. They look like the sea life of my world, only more varied.

As I'm watching, a shark-like beast with several mouths and one giant eye chases an animal that looks like a cross between a seal and a deer. The predator runs down its prey and rips it to shreds. Clouds of scavengers move in quickly and finish off the scraps that the shark leaves behind.

"Are we safe?" I ask nervously. There are more of the sharks around, and other mutations that look even fiercer.

"They won't harm us," Art says. "This is a perfectly balanced world. Nothing would attack anything that it was not, by nature, designed to prey upon."

As he says that, a sea snake the size of a redwood tree passes beneath us. It raises its huge head and studies us. I feel like I'm going to be its lunch. But then it moves on, jaws opening and closing slowly, in search of other food.

"I don't like this," I mutter. "When can we leave?"

"Soon," Art says. "First I must acknowledge the greeting of the natives."

A ring of creatures closes around us. Each looks like a cross between a small whale and an octopus, large but graceful. Their many arms are adorned with shells and sea flowers, and intricate designs which might be tattoos. They swirl over, under and around one another, as if dancing.

"They *are* dancing," Art says. "They worship my kind and wish to perform in our honour. We have not passed through here in a long time. They are excited."

"Why do they think so much of you?" I ask.

"We saved them from a demon attack long ago."

"The Demonata cross to other worlds?" I frown.

"Of course," Art says. "They hate all life forms. You are not the first to suffer at their hands. And you won't be the last. Far from it."

Other creatures gather round us, joining the dance. Their movements become more involved, dozens of different species sweeping around one another, every blink of an eye or swish of a tail carefully choreographed. Through the crush I spot something weird rising from the depths.

"Is that a chess board?" I ask. It's much bigger than any board I've ever seen, but it's the right shape, with the usual arrangement of black and white squares.

"There are Boards like this on almost all the worlds where we have had an influence," Art says. "The Boards are central to the development of intelligence. Some species forget about them as they evolve, but most remember in one way or another."

"I don't get it. What's the big deal about chess?"

"The game means nothing," Art answers. "The *Board* is everything."

Something about the way he stresses the word sparks a memory. I recall a visit I paid to Lord Loss's kingdom several years ago. The demon master loves chess. One of the rooms in his web-based castle was full of sets. He produced a board which he referred to as the Original Board. Each square was a self-contained universe of its own, filled with an array of demons.

"Yes," Art says before I can form a question. "That was the Board we used on your world."

"I still don't understand," I frown. "The Board was just a toy."

"The Boards are not toys," Art says. "Each is a map of the original universe, a link to the past before time."

"You're talking gibberish," I scowl.

"It will become clear soon," Art assures me, then pushes through a gap that the sea creatures have created. "Come. I am fully rested, and the dance has moved into its final arc. It is time for us to depart."

# TAKING TO THE SKIES

→We skip from one world to another, chamber to chamber, through the sub-universe of strange lights. I try to figure out how the windows are being opened, hoping to use the information to break free and make my way back home. But I don't know how Art gets the panels to pulse and merge.

"Tell me about yourself," I suggest, partly to break the monotony, partly to learn more about my mysterious guide.

"What do you wish to know?" he replies.

"Where are you from? Beranabus only said that the Old Creatures were beings of ancient, powerful magic, who left our world long ago."

"We leave every planet eventually," Art sighs. "We are nomads, moving from one world to another, never settling."

"But you must have a home," I press. "Everyone comes from somewhere."

"Not us," Art says. "We are of the original universe. We had no beginning."

"That doesn't make sense," I grunt.

"It will–" Art begins.

"*–soon*," I finish sarcastically.

"Sorry," Art says. "I know this is hard. But there is much we have to tell you and it is complicated."

"Let's try something simpler then." I think about the sort of things I'd ask any stranger. "How old are you?"

Art makes a sound like someone clearing their throat.

"Oh, come on!" I shout. "Surely you can tell me that much."

"There is no easy answer," Art says. "We are as old as this universe but we existed before it. In the original universe, there was no such thing as time. We were not born. We did not age. We simply *were*."

"You can't be as old as the universe," I challenge him. "It's billions of years old. Nothing lives for that long."

"We do," Art insists. "We exist as spheres of light, and light is almost ageless."

"*Almost?* You're not immortal?"

"Not any more," Art says.

"This is crazy," I mutter.

"Be patient," Art urges. "By the end of this journey we'll reveal the secrets of the universe, the origins of life and the cause of the Big Bang."

"What's the Big Bang?"

Art is silent for a long time. Then, in a dejected tone, he says, "This is going to be harder than we thought."

→More worlds and chambers. I doze during some of the journey. In the demon universe I can go weeks or months without sleep, but here I grow tired, just as I do on Earth. I start to wonder how long we've been travelling.

"This is the fourth day," Art answers.

"How much longer will it take?"

"I cannot say."

"A week?" I snap. "A month? Years?" I lick my lips and ask quietly, "You *will* take me back, won't you?"

There's a pause. "If you choose to return, we–"

"What do you mean?" I roar. "Of course I'll return! Why shouldn't I? Are you going to try to–"

"Peace," Art hushes me. "The choice will be yours. I don't think you'll want to go back, but we will not prevent you from following your destiny."

"I'll definitely want to go back," I growl.

"You should not make such sweeping statements," Art says. "When you went in search of the demon masquerading as your brother, you were certain you'd return home when you found him, but you didn't. There are no certainties except death. And even that–"

Whatever he was about to say is lost, because we pass through a window into a chamber made of moss-covered stones. And the place is crawling with demons.

They're foul beasts, shaped like horses, but their flesh is rotting away and their bones poke through. Yellow blood drips down their legs from their rib cages. The heads are larger than on any horse I've seen, and each has two sets of mouths, one above the other. There are no teeth — instead, human-looking fingernails jut out of their gums, blood and drool dribbling between the cracks.

The demons had been fighting or playing with each other – hard to tell with these monsters – but they stop when we pop out in the middle of them. Then, with howls of hunger and delight, they hurl themselves at us.

I react automatically and fire a ball of energy at the nearest beast, then leap clear, on to one of the higher stones of the chamber. The roof caved in long ago and I can see out. A quick survey of the land beyond reveals a scorched, ruined world teeming with monsters. A massive demon is rising into the air a few miles away. Hundreds of beasts are clinging to it, or settled on its back in rows. Fleshy strands dangle from its stomach. Large rocks are attached to the lower ends.

A horse-demon jumps, rears its hooves and slashes at my throat. I duck, slam my shoulder into its face and knock it back. "Art!" I scream as others come pounding closer.

"Cover your eyes," Art says. "Use magic as well as your hands."

"What good will that do?" I yell, jumping to another stone.

There's a flash of light and my eyes melt in their sockets. The pain is intense but nothing new. It's just like when my original eyes were stabbed out.

As I howl and fight off waves of pain and madness, Art says, "You should have done what I told you. These demons are called the Sligstata. Light is my only weapon against them. Most can construct new eyes, as you can, but you have done it before, so you should be faster. Set to work immediately, but focus your other senses on the Sligstata. You can avoid them if you concentrate."

"But I can't see!" I howl. "I'm blind!"

"You'll be dead if you don't do what I tell you," Art snarls. There's real fear in his tone. "I can't fight these creatures, even if I turn into Artery — there are too many. I can blind them again, but they'll soon grow wise to that trick. I'm opening a new window but it will take a few minutes. You must defend yourself."

I curse the Old Creature, then set to work on

building a new pair of eyes. It was a long, complicated process before, but this time they grow swiftly, smoothly.

As the eyes form, I listen to the demons and sense their positions. They're stumbling around, lashing out at one another, wild with blind panic. No threat as long as I remain up here. But others are coming. They swarm over the ruins of the chamber, knocking each other aside in their eagerness to tear into me, the echo of their hooves ringing louder as they draw closer.

There's strong magic in the air. I let a ball of power build in my fists and wait until the monsters are several feet away, packed tight, focused on me. Then I let them have it, a blast straight down the middle, scattering them, ripping open stomachs and heads, incinerating eyes, faces and internal organs.

The demons screech with pain and anger, falling beneath the hooves of those behind them. One of the Sligstata hurls itself at me, both sets of mouths gnashing, fingernails twitching. I pirouette away from it like a ballet dancer and end up on the opposite side of the chamber. My eyes have almost completed the healing process, but I still can't see.

"Protect yourself," Art hisses. I was letting another ball of magic build in my hands, but now I divert the power to my eyes and erect a wall of blackness. I see nothing but I know when the light flashes by the screams of the Sligstata.

One of the beasts must have expected the flash and guarded its eyes, because while the others thrash around and topple into the chamber, it makes a beeline for me. No time to dance aside. Planting my feet firmly, I grab the monster by its neck and hold its spitting mouths a few inches from my throat. The stench of its breath would floor a lesser mortal.

As I'm struggling with the demon, my eyes connect with my brain and the world swims back into sight. The Sligstata's mouths are closer than I thought. Gritting my teeth, I push hard and its jaws slide back. But it's tenacious and my fingers are damp with sweat and blood. In a few seconds it will wriggle forward and finish me off.

When I first tried to fight in the Demonata's universe, I was so scared I threw up. I was ashamed at the time, but since then I've learnt the value of a good stream of vomit. I send a magical buzz down my throat and a wave of digested food rises. I spray the demon with hot, thick puke. It gurgles happily, then screeches as I turn the liquid to acid. As the Sligstata burns and writhes, I drop it and look around.

Dozens of fresh demons are racing towards the chamber. Too many to fight. Some of those beneath me have grown new eyes and are knocking aside the blind Sligstata, zoning in on me, hell-bent on making me pay for their torment.

"It's looking bad," I yell at Art, firing a magical bolt at a demon as it tops the chamber wall, driving it back.

"A few more seconds," Art says calmly, pulsing steadily, hovering in the air above my head.

"We don't have that long."

"Just keep them busy a couple more..."

A blue window blinks into life. I don't wait for Art to give the order. With a yell of fear and triumph, I throw myself at it, linking my hands like a person diving into a swimming pool. The Sligstata snap at me with their nightmarish mouths, but miss, and a second later I'm flying through the panel of light. I start to cheer but the sound catches in my throat as fingernails bite into my left leg. I kick but the beast holds firm and drags me back. The patches of light are twinkling seductively but I'm being hauled away from them, back into the chamber of death.

I try summoning magic to fry the Sligstata, but I'm temporarily drained. This looks like the end of Cornelius Fleck. I just hope they kill me quickly. Some demons can keep their victims alive for thousands of–

A crackle of electricity shoots through my leg. It sets my skin tingling but hurts the demon more. It starts to lose its grip. I glance back and see that the Old Creature has once again taken on the shape of Artery. The fire in the green-skinned demon's right eye socket narrows then expands — he's winking at me! Then he grabs hold of me and leaps. We shoot forward and the window snaps shut behind us. Art transforms back into a ball of light and wraps around me. We swoop towards the pulsing lights like a pair of birds, laughing hysterically at our narrow escape.

# GOING UNIVERSAL

→It takes a while to settle down. "Thanks," I say when I've stopped chuckling. "You saved my life."

"That's my job," Art says wryly.

"I thought I was done for. There were so many of them…" I frown. "That wasn't the demon universe, was it?"

"No," Art says. "I told you we would not be crossing to their realm."

"Then what were the Sligstata doing there?"

"That world was demon-free a few months ago," Art says. "They must have broken through recently. I wouldn't have come this way if I'd known."

"Even so, how could so many…" I stop as the answer pops into my head. "They opened a tunnel between their universe and that world."

"Yes," Art says.

"The sky demon," I say slowly. "Did you see it?"

"Yes. There were more, a convoy of them in the sky."

"Where were they going?"

"Other worlds." Art sighs. "There were stones of

magic hanging beneath it. You call them lodestones. We set such markers in place on all the worlds we visit. They help us hold the Demonata at bay and give the inhabitants of the planets a chance to evolve.

"The defensive power of the stones fades when we move on. As the safety net crumbles, demons seek to open windows and tunnels. If they succeed, they wipe the world clean. Then, in most cases, they return to their own universe. But sometimes on a world where lodestones are plentiful, they use it as a base to launch more attacks.

"The sky demon and its passengers are heading for neighbouring worlds, using the stolen, corrupted magic of the lodestones to sustain them. It will take millennia, but they are patient. The power will drain from the stones eventually and they'll have to return home, but that might not be for millions of years."

"And as long as the stones hold, they can stay in this universe?" I ask, feeling sick.

"Yes."

"How far is that sky demon from Earth?"

"Billions of miles. It will never trouble your people."

"But if it was setting off from a nearer world, like Atlantis, it could descend on us one day, carrying hordes of demons?"

"Yes," Art says.

"Is our universe full of sky demons, slowly making their way from one world to the next?"

"Hardly *full of*," Art mutters. "But there are many of them."

"Then we can't beat them," I croak. "We thought if we stopped them crossing, we were safe. But if armies are already here, making their way towards us…"

"All worlds will fall eventually," Art says glumly. "All beings will die. That is the nature of the universe. Nothing is forever. Death claims all things in the end."

"Sure," I grunt bitterly. "But I didn't know there were scores of demons cruising the skies, working hard to wipe us out."

"It is not an issue," Art says. "Your world will have fallen long before any sky demon reaches it."

My eyes narrow. "What are you talking about?"

"The lodestones are a temporary form of protection," he says. "Demons always cross. The only hope any beings have is to master the skies. If a species learns to move on to other worlds, they can stay ahead of the Demonata. Your people haven't made that crucial step to the stars. Your planet will fall within the next year. It is inescapable."

My jaw drops, then firmly closes. I breathe in and out through my nostrils, waiting until I'm calm. When I'm in control, I say very clearly, "I want to go home."

"It would be pointless," Art says. "You could do nothing to stop it."

"I have to try. Even if I fail, I want to be there at the end. If Earth's going to fall, I'll fall with it."

"No," Art says. "You have a greater destiny."

"I don't care about–" I begin to snarl.

"Life must continue," Art interrupts. "We realised, billions of years ago, that this universe was doomed. The Demonata are stronger than those who populate our worlds. In time they'll conquer all. We devoted ourselves to denying them that victory. We vowed to find a way to ensure life continued."

"I thought you said all things perish."

"Ultimately," he replies. "This universe is a living thing, and it will die of old age eventually. But we can make sure that the end comes in its own time, not at the hands of the Demonata. *If* you help us."

I'm silent a long time. I can't understand everything Art is talking about, but if he's right... if there's some way to thwart the plans of the Demonata...

"How much further do we have to go?" I ask.

"Not far," Art says. "Another day, perhaps, and we will reach the Crux."

"And you'll tell me everything?" I press. "No more riddles or half-answers?"

"Everything will be revealed," Art promises. "After

that you can stay or go as you please."

"Then I'll come," I sigh, and although my intentions are good, it feels like I've just sold my soul to the devil — or worse.

# THE CRUX

→More worlds and chambers. Pretty much all of the planets have fallen. They feel old and cold. Art says these were some of the earliest settled worlds, the first planets that the Old Creatures populated.

"You're like gods," I mutter. "You spread life across the universe."

"We nurture life," Art corrects me. "We don't create it. We don't know where the living things of this universe came from, how life was born out of fire and chaos. There are forces at work beyond even our knowledge."

"Then gods – or God – might be real?" I press.

"Perhaps."

"What about an afterlife?" I ask. "Do you know what happens to our souls when we die?"

"No," Art says. "We will talk more about that later, but first…"

We're approaching a small window. We've been moving at a constant speed, but now Art slows.

"We are almost at the Crux," he says and there's a nervous edge to his voice. I feel the ball of light tighten around me.

"What are you doing?" I ask suspiciously.

"The Crux is a place of great danger," he replies. "We cannot stay long, and I must cling tightly to you while we're there, or you will be disintegrated."

"Hold on!" I yelp. "You never said anything about disintegration!"

"I didn't want to frighten you," Art chuckles.

I stare anxiously at the window, wondering if there's anything I can do to stop this.

"Don't be afraid," Art says. "I know what I'm doing."

"Wait!" I cry as we draw close. "Have you ever taken anyone like me into the Crux before?"

Art hesitates, then says sheepishly, "No."

"Then how do you know–"

Before I can finish, we smash through the window and I scream at the top of my voice, as if riding the wildest rollercoaster in the universe.

→As soon as we slip through the window, the temperature skyrockets. We're gliding towards a massive orb of seething fire. This must be what the sun is like close up. The space around us throbs with magical energy. I sense Art tapping into that magic, using it to shield us from the unbelievable heat, glare and radiation. I can't imagine anything non-magical surviving here.

We zip closer to the ball of fire. It shimmers savagely as I stare at it, awestruck and horrified. It doesn't have a constant shape. The edges buckle and warp, bulge out, then twist back in on themselves. Pillars of flame shoot from the surface, spiral around the face of the orb and are absorbed by it again. Sometimes it turns a blinding white shade. Other times it goes black and becomes almost invisible against the expanse of space around it. Most of the time it flickers between the two colours, waves of fire lashing across the surface and bubbling over without pause.

The sun-like ball terrifies me. It's not just the heat. Being here is wrong. I feel like I'm breaking a sacred law by looking at this wild globe of wondrous fire.

"We've broken more laws than you could imagine by bringing you here," Art says. "But we cannot always be prisoners of the laws we live by. Sometimes we have to transcend them."

We press closer to the orb. We're almost upon it. My mouth is dry. My skin feels like it's burning. My eyes seem to be roasting in their sockets. I want to turn and get as far away from here as possible. But before I can beg Art to stop, we hit the outer rim and are swallowed by a billion licks of ravenous flame.

→It takes several minutes to cut through the outer ring. I've fought demons made of fire, so a realm of flames is nothing new. But this fire is hotter than any I've experienced. It roars about us like a living, furious sea. But Art holds firm and guides me through the billowing walls of the furnace.

Finally we break through the flames and enter a realm of bewitching marvels. It's a vast, oval, grey space, illuminated by constant bolts of lightning. There's debris everywhere, asteroids, pebbles and dust swirling around. The lightning regularly splits rocks and splinters them, but the pieces join with other shards to form new, larger rocks, which in turn are split again.

The space is dominated by a series of enormous square panels. Half are black, half white. The panels revolve slowly around the sphere, never meeting. Anything that hits the panels – lightning forks, rocks, flickers of flame – is absorbed, then spat out moments later.

Balls of multicoloured light – Old Creatures – float around the black panels. Hundreds of demons cluster around the white squares. My insides tense when I spot the Demonata but Art speaks quickly to calm me.

"They Will Not Harm Us," he says. "This Place Is Sacred To Both Sides. We Do Not Kill Here."

"You could have warned me earlier," I growl, then frown. "What happened to your voice? It's deeper than before, and echoey."

"We Are All Speaking To You Now," Art says stiffly. "We Do Not Experience Individuality When We Are Together."

I glance around at the various balls of light. They were pulsing in unison as Art spoke. It's too confusing to think of them all speaking at the same time, so I focus on Art and pretend I'm talking to a single entity.

"What's the story?" I ask, shivering as a bolt of lightning strikes the film of light around me and is deflected. "Why are we here? What are the big secrets?"

"The Panels Are The Key," Art says. "You Remember The Chess Board We Saw On The Earlier World?"

"Yes, but what does..." I stop and cast an eye over the panels again, doing a quick count. There are thirty-two black squares and an equal number of white.

"The Original Universe Was Shaped Like A Chess Board," Art explains. "There Were Sixty-Four Zones, Half Black, Half White. Each Zone Was Limitless In Size. Time Did Not Exist. The Universe Had Existed

And Would Exist Forever. It Was The Same For Us And The Demonata."

"I don't understand," I interrupt. "Everything has to begin somewhere."

"Only If Time Exists," Art corrects me.

"How can time *not* exist?" I huff.

"Time As You Know It Began With The Big Bang."

"I told you I don't know what that means."

"Peace," Art calms me. "We Will Come To That. First, Accept That This Was The State Of The Universe. Sixty-Four Zones, Equal In All Respects, Black Separated From White By A Force We Called The Kah-Gash."

I focus intently when he mentions the Kah-Gash, ignoring the things I don't understand. I can try to make sense of the bewildering bits later.

"Demons Existed In The White Zones," Art continues. "Vile, Violent Monsters Who Could Reproduce. We Inhabited The Black Zones And Were Sterile. That Did Not Trouble Us. Since There Was No Time, We Were Immortal. Death Did Exist – We *Could* Be Killed – But It Rarely Bothered Us. We Roamed The Endless Depths Of Our Zones, Peaceful And Content.

"Demons And Old Creatures Were Never Meant To Mix. The Kah-Gash Kept Us Separate."

I spot a disturbance among a group of demons clustered around one of the white panels. Until a few seconds ago, they swarmed around the panel like ants, but now they part, forming two neat ranks. One of the beasts glides between the others, angles for the panel, then brushes against it and is absorbed. I wait for it to emerge, but nothing happens.

"The Demon Is Dead," Art says. "It Was Ancient, One Of Those Who Existed In The Original Universe. No Living Creature Can Touch The Panels And Survive. Most Of The Original Demonata And Old Creatures Choose To Perish Here When It Is Their Time."

"One down, just a few trillion to go," I chuckle humourlessly. Then I pause. "Is that why the other demons are here, to bid farewell to the dead one?"

"Yes."

"I didn't think demons worked that way. Those I've known don't care about any of the others."

"The Original Demons Are Different," Art says. "They Have Known Each Other For So Long That They Have Formed Bonds. We Would Normally Stay Away At A Time Like This, As They Do When We Gather Here For A Funeral. But It Was Important To Protect You."

"I thought you said you don't kill here."

"We Don't," Art says. "But If They See A Human, They Might Attack. We Will Distract Them If They Grow Curious, And Defend You If Necessary."

We watch the end of the ceremony. Nothing much happens. The demons hold their ranks for a while, then break apart and drift towards the ring of fire which encircles the Crux.

"Initially We Were Not Aware Of The Demonata And They Knew Nothing Of Us," Art resumes. "But The Demonata Were Curious. They Tested The Barriers Where White Met Black, And Found A Way To Cross. They Discovered Us."

"And they attacked," I guess. "They set out to kill you all."

Art sighs. "We Knew Nothing Of War. We Fled For The Furthest Reaches Of Our Zones, Hoping The Demonata Would Lose Interest And Let Us Be."

"Some hope!" I snort.

"It Was Brutal," Art says softly. "We Learnt About Pain, Suffering And Loss For The First Time. We Were Innocent, But We Matured Fast. We Had To Or They Would Have Slain Us All.

"We Fought Back. Your People Know Much Of Warfare, But They Have Never Seen It On Such A Scale. Universal, Timeless, A War Of Magic. The Universe Burned. The Kah-Gash Buckled. Ultimately It Could Stand The Strain No Longer."

We've been drifting closer to one of the black squares. It's bigger than I assumed, several miles high. I feel tiny as we pass within its shadow.

"We Knew We Should Stop," Art whispers. "The Laws Were Shattering. The Universe Was Crumbling. The Kah-Gash Could Not Hold. But Still We Fought. We Had Become Slaves To War.

"In The End The Kah-Gash Fractured. In A Blinding, Destructive Flash, All Sixty-Four Zones Shrank To The Size Of A Speck. A Split-Second Later, The Ball Of The Universe Exploded. Everything Was Destroyed And Reborn. Life As You Know It Began."

"And that's when the universe was created?" I ask.

"*Universes*," Art corrects me. "There Are Two. Although There Were Sixty-Four Zones Before The Big Bang, There Was Only One Universe. The Laws Of The White Zones Differed To Those Of The Black, But They Were Held In Place By The Kah-Gash. Now The Two Universes Are Separate."

"I don't understand why they exist at all," I mutter. "Why wasn't everything wiped out in the explosion?"

"The Kah-Gash Protected Us. Its Last Act Was To Create Two Individual Universes, Dividing The Warring Races. It Hoped The New Structures Would Keep Us Apart. As You Have Seen, They Did Not."

"OK," I say slowly. "Our universe and the Demonata's were born out of the ashes of the old one, like a phoenix rising from the flames after it dies. So what's this place?"

"This Is The Crux, The One Point Common To Both

Universes. The Explosion Happened Here. The New Universes Spread Out In All Directions From This Area. The Universes Overlap Each Other. They Share The Same Space But Never Touch. Except Here. The Crux Exists In Both Universes At Once."

"And those black and white panels are the remains of the Kah-Gash?"

"Yes, But Only Of Its Body. All Conscious Beings Have A Body And A Soul. What You See Here Are The Kah-Gash's Physical Remains. The Segments Of Its Soul Flew Off Along With Everything Else."

"Does that mean there are sixty-four pieces?" I ask.

"No. There Are Only Three. You, Bec And..." Art falls silent, then says, "Something Is Happening."

"What do you–" I start to ask.

"Quiet!" Art snaps.

I look around, trying to determine the source of Art's unease. My first thought is that the demons are mounting an attack, but they don't seem to be paying any attention to us. And the panels are revolving the same as before. So why...

Wait. I'm wrong. The panels aren't the same. They're not circling any longer. They're gliding forward now. Towards us. Towards *me*.

"Art?" I mumble. "What are they doing?"

"Gravitating Towards You. Possibly Trying To Reunite."

"Is that bad?" I ask.

Art doesn't answer. Instead he reverses direction and suddenly we're flying towards the ring of fire as fast as we can.

"What's going on?" I shout.

"We Do Not Know," Art says. "We Had Not Expected Such A Reaction."

"What will happen if they join?"

"We Are Not Sure. Maybe Nothing. Maybe The End Of All We Know."

"The end of the universes?" I gasp.

"Perhaps."

I stare with horror at the giant squares. They're coming together slowly, but not slowly enough for my liking.

"Will they stop if we get out of here?" I ask.

"We Think So," Art says. There's a brief pause. "We *Hope* So."

I watch helplessly as we draw away from the panels. It looks like we'll make it out of here before they join. After that we'll just have to pray that –

A blast of magic strikes us and Art makes a high-pitched shrieking noise. We're knocked sideways. I glance to my left, the direction the shot came from. I spot a pack of demons streaking towards us. They unleash more bolts of magic, but the Old Creatures intercept them and blast them aside or absorb the shots themselves.

"Art?" I whisper, fearing the worst.

"I Am Not Dead," he says. "You Will Perish Too If I Die."

We pick up speed again.

"Why are they doing this?" I pant, keeping a close eye on the fighting. The Old Creatures and demons aren't engaging at close quarters – they hover apart and take long-range shots at one another – but it looks ugly. A few of the balls of light are shattered while I watch, and several of the demons are ripped apart.

"The Demonata Wish For The End Of The Universes," Art says. "They Must Have Seen The Panels Move, Spotted You And Guessed You Were The Source Of The Disturbance. Like Us, They Cannot Know What Will Happen If The Panels Join, But They Clearly Wish To Keep You Here And–"

Art is struck again. He doesn't slow this time, but his scream lasts even longer than before. We're almost at the ring of fire, but a demon has broken through the ranks of Old Creatures and is narrowing the gap, moving faster than we are.

We hit the wall of fire and plough through. It feels even hotter than it did the last time. Areas of my skin start to smoulder.

"You Must Use Magic," Art says calmly. "I Cannot Protect You As I Did Before. I Am Wounded And Must Focus On Opening A Window."

"If we make it through the fire, we'll be safe, right?" I yell, doing what I can to counter the burns breaking out across my flesh. "They can't follow us into the human universe, can they?"

"No," Art says. "But We Will Not Make It. The Demon Will Catch Us. We Have To Open The Window From Here."

"Can you do that?" I ask.

"In Theory," he says, doing nothing to calm my frayed nerves.

Art is struck again, but pushes on, concentrating on the small patches of light which I glimpse through the flicker of the flames. I try to create a barrier to help but there isn't a strong supply of magic here, at least not the sort I can tap into. The best I can do is cool my skin and quench the worst of the flames.

The demon looks nothing like those I've fought in the past. It's huge, a mass of bulges, not shaped like any animal I've ever seen. I'm not even sure where its face is. All I know is that it's utterly evil, determined to kill us and closing quickly.

"Art..." I mutter.

"We Know," he replies. "I Have Almost..."

A window of red light forms in the distance, almost impossible to see against the fiery backdrop. I give a shout of triumph, but it's drowned out when another blast of magic hits us. Art screeches. The bolt of energy drives us closer towards the window, but Art's scream cuts out midway and the lights around me shatter.

I realise with horror that Art has been killed, but there's no time to mourn. My flesh erupts, fire exploding from every pore. I scream silently, consumed by flames. In a mad fury I try to slap them out. It's a hopeless task, but before the fire can finish the job, I hit the window and plunge into the sub-universe of multicoloured lights without anyone to protect or guide me.

# NEW FACE, OLD STORY

→There's no oxygen, so the flames die away. The pain doesn't, but I've no time to focus on that. It's freezing and there isn't any air. If I can't construct a shell around myself, and swiftly, I'm finished.

I search for magic, but there's nothing I can make use of. This zone of lights contains even less magical energy than there was on Earth. I thrash about like a fish on dry land, lips shut, eyes bulging. I feel my skin tighten from the cold but that doesn't bother me. I'll suffocate long before I freeze to death.

As my lungs strain for air that isn't there, my limbs go still and a calm wave spreads through me. In a way this is fitting. I was always a lonely child. I often felt out of place, not in sync with the people around me. Now I'm going to die in true isolation, more alone than any human has ever been.

A gloomy mist crosses my eyes. I think it's the shades of death drawing over my face, but then I blink and realise it's a dark green window which has opened ahead of me. As I stare at it numbly, a ball of light shoots through and envelops me from head to toe. I've just enough time to marvel at the warmth it brings. Then my eyelids flutter and I fall unconscious.

→I awake on a grey, cold, ashen world. I sit up, groaning. My skin is blistered. Parts feel raw. But I'm alive.

Something moves nearby.

"Art?" I call.

"No." A tall black man steps into view. He's fat, with very dark skin, dressed in an expensive-looking suit.

My eyes widen. "*Raz*?" I gasp.

"Only in appearance," the man says solemnly.

"I don't understand." I start to rise, but pain prevents me. Grimacing, I frown at the fat man. Raz Warlo was a Disciple. I met him when I first joined Beranabus. He was killed during the quest to find my baby brother. "Why change?" I wheeze.

"The one you knew as Art is dead," Raz says. "Although shapes mean nothing to us, we know you need them to make sense of the universe. We felt it would be easier for you if I took a different form." He looks down at himself and frowns. "The suit was a difficult touch."

"What happened back there?" I ask.

"The panels of the Kah-Gash reacted to your presence," Raz says. "The demons attacked. We managed to get you out before they killed you."

"And the panels? Did they stop?"

"The fact that we still exist makes me think so," Raz says drily.

I nod slowly, then clear my throat. "Art sacrificed himself to save me."

"Evidently."

"And you placed your life at risk by coming after me."

"Yes."

"*Why?*" I groan. "Why take me to the Crux and risk your lives for my sake?"

"That will become clear very soon," Raz says and nods at a rock behind me. "That is a lodestone. It is the reason I brought you to this world. I suggest you use its power to heal yourself before we continue."

Now that I focus, I realise there's a strong current of magic flowing around me. I tap into it gratefully and set to work on my wounds, patching up the holes burnt in my flesh.

As I'm sealing the last of the gashes, Raz looks around at the dead land, then says, "Did you ever plan to have children?"

The question throws me and I squint at him. "I

hadn't given it much thought. Probably not. It's hard to bring up a child when you're busy battling demons."

"The Old Creatures can't reproduce," Raz says. "It didn't matter in the original universe, since we were immortal. That changed when the Kah-Gash fractured. Now every creature ages. We are captives of time and the price of our captivity is death."

As Raz speaks, I stand and stretch. My stomach rumbles. I'm ravenous and thirsty, but there's nothing to eat or drink, so I do my best to ignore the cries of my deprived body and focus on the Old Creature's lecture.

"We accepted our mortality," Raz continues, "but the Demonata craved a return to the way things were. They wanted to live forever. So they set about thwarting the hold of death."

"How?" I frown.

"As long as the new universes exist, death will claim us all," Raz says. "But if those universes are eradicated… if the Kah-Gash is reassembled and the old laws are re-established…"

I start to tremble. "Beranabus said the Kah-Gash could destroy a universe. But you're saying it could destroy *both?*"

"Yes. The Kah-Gash could draw everything back through time to the moment of the Big Bang, eliminate all that has happened since and restore the original universe."

"What would happen to us?" I gasp.

"You would have never existed," Raz says. "Time would be reversed. All the creatures and planets of the new universes would be wiped out. Only the Old Creatures and the Demonata would survive."

"Why wouldn't you be killed too?"

"We think we would be protected, as we were when the Kah-Gash exploded. If we are correct, even the new Demonata – the spawn of the original beasts – would be spared, since they carry the genes of their parents."

"Then why not us?" I ask hollowly.

"You are not our offspring," Raz says sadly. "New life was created when this universe was born. We have guided many species and helped souls develop. But you are not ours.

"We must go," Raz says abruptly. "You need to eat, so we will move on." He sets to work on the tiny patches of light in the air around us.

"What world of wonders are we heading for now?" I ask.

"We're not going to a world," Raz says. "We are going to a *spaceship*."

# PICKING UP THE PIECES

→I wanted to be an astronaut when I was younger, walk on the moon, fly around in a rocket, zap aliens with a laser gun, teleport across galaxies. I've done a lot more than that in the years since, boldly going to places where no man would ever *want* to go. Still, that love of spacemen and rockets remains, and when Raz tells me we're heading for a spaceship, I fill with excitement. But when we slide through the window, it's into a large room of concrete walls, boxes stacked neatly at the sides, fluorescent lights overhead. There's a small garden in the middle of the room.

"This isn't a spaceship," I grumble. "Spaceships are made of metal, full of stuff like..." I stop, realising how ridiculous that sounds. Spaceships in movies and comics might be like that. But in the real world, built by beings of another planet, why should they be?

"Precisely," Raz says. "This is a massive craft designed to navigate the vastness of space. It is the size of a city, home to two million creatures. They fled their dying planet long ago and have sailed among the stars ever since.

"Now eat."

"Eat what?" I ask, looking around.

"Anything," Raz says. "The crates are packed with nutritious substances. And there are bottles of liquid in those." He points at the boxes to my left.

"Won't anyone mind?" I ask nervously, not wanting to get on the wrong side of short-tempered aliens.

"These are excess supplies. Nobody will notice."

I shuffle over to the crates and lift off the lid of the nearest box. There are large plastic bottles inside. The liquid in them is an unpleasant green colour. The stench, when I snap the top off, is vile.

"Are you sure this is safe?" I ask.

"Yes."

"Why aren't you drinking any?"

"I don't need it."

Sceptical, I raise the bottle and take a sip. It's disgusting! I spit it out and grimace, then reluctantly drain a mouthful and swish it around. The taste doesn't improve, but after half a minute of swishing, I gulp, then lower the bottle and wait to be sick. When nothing happens, I drink some more, then look for something to sink my teeth into. The food is as unappealing as the liquid, but it fills me up. When my stomach can hold no more, I wipe my lips with a hand and glance at Raz.

"Done?" he asks.

"Done," I confirm.

"Are you ready to go on a quick tour?"

"Can I?" I ask eagerly.

"I know you want to. I can disguise us to look like natives."

"Great! Let's do it."

Leaving the storeroom, we walk down a long corridor, then take an elevator to an upper level. It looks remarkably like the elevators on Earth.

"You shouldn't be surprised," Raz says. "We sowed the seeds of intelligence among most of the universe's beings, and the rest were assisted by those we first helped. There are many similarities between species."

The elevator comes to a halt and the doors slide open. I step out into a noisy street that could be in any of Earth's busier cities. Buildings like ours, vehicles that look like cars, streetlamps and power cables. The only difference is that instead of a sky, there's another level overhead. Otherwise it's unnervingly familiar.

The same can't be said for the *people*. They have no human traits. Long tendrils instead of arms and legs. Their faces, which are in the middle of their bodies, have several gloopy eyes set in a semi-circle around a small, toothless mouth. No ears or nose. Each is a mix of colours. They're slimy, dripping freely as they pass. Smaller creatures feast on the mucous, an army of insect-like slime-eaters who gobble it up, keeping the paths clean.

I stare for a long time at the aliens, then glance at Raz and myself and frown. "We don't look any different. I thought you were going to disguise us."

"I haven't altered our bodies," Raz says. "I'm affecting the visual sensors of those around us, so that to their eyes we appear as they do. Yes," he adds with a grin before I can say anything, "that *is* pretty cool."

We wander down the street. I peer in windows as we pass, and even enter a few of the buildings, trying to figure out what the stores are selling, what the creatures are doing, what the buildings are for. Raz whispers in my ear as we wind our way down the street, then turn into another, and another, exploring.

"When the Kah-Gash split, the pieces of its soul shot off ahead of the blast, travelling faster than light or any of the other forces unleashed by the explosion. They darted in and out of the new universes, passing from one to the other as they flew further apart.

"Eventually they slowed and drifted. Sometimes they floated across realms like cosmic butterflies. Other times they disappeared from one part of a universe and popped up on the opposite side in the blink of an eye.

"The patches of light you have seen since birth are physical remnants of the Kah-Gash. There were barriers of energy and magic between the squares of the original universe. When the Kah-Gash exploded, the barriers shattered, but their fragments were used to stitch the fabric of the new universes together. It took us a long time to realise that, since we cannot see them."

"You can't see the lights?" I frown.

"No," Raz says. "They only reveal themselves to the eyes of the Kah-Gash."

"I don't understand."

"There are three parts of the Kah-Gash," Raz says. "The trigger, memory and eyes. The trigger is the commanding force. The memory stores all that happens. The eyes see the hidden strings which bind the universes in place.

"This only became clear to us over the long course of time. In the beginning we didn't know how many pieces there were, what function they played, where they'd gone. We were not even sure that parts of the Kah-Gash still existed.

"The Demonata knew no more than we did, but threw themselves into the search. Their desperate plan was to find the parts of the Kah-Gash, reassemble them and restore the original universe. It's a plan they haven't wavered from.

"For a time we saw no threat. We thought it was a fool's quest. But then the parts began to reappear. They had the ability to turn up anywhere, in a comet, a rock, a tree, an animal, even in one of the new demons. The pieces never merged with any of the Old Creatures or original demons, but all other forms were fair game. They caused no harm, existing in harmony with their hosts, but their re-emergence filled us with panic."

Raz shivers, then continues. "The Demonata pursued the pieces with a mad passion. When they finally found one, they experimented, seeking ways to harness its power. They found they could influence its destination when it moved from one form to another, ensuring it stayed within their grasp.

"The demons searched hard for the other pieces. They couldn't cross from their universe to ours, but they didn't need to. The parts of the Kah-Gash passed freely between universes. The Demonata could wait, even though it might take billions of years."

We come to another elevator and ride it down to a random lower level. I find a park, full of strangely shaped trees and bushes. I dodge between them as Raz speaks.

"We couldn't let them reunite the Kah-Gash," Raz says. "We felt responsible for this universe's new life forms. They were simple creatures, but they had a right to exist. So we counter-plotted. Although the demons couldn't cross universes, we had the power to enter theirs. We launched a raiding party. After a brief battle, we freed the piece of the Kah-Gash and fled. The Demonata couldn't follow. All they could do was keep searching and waiting.

"That's how things continued over millions of years," Raz says, as if talking about the passing of a couple of weeks. "The Demonata imprisoned pieces of the Kah-Gash. We crossed, fought and freed them."

"Are you stronger than the demons?" I ask.

"No," Raz says. "But we only needed to destroy the form in which a piece was stuck. When that happened, it shot free. If the demons had been able to focus, they could have directed it into another form of their choosing, but we distracted them.

"We also searched for pieces in our universe," Raz goes on. "We had no wish to reassemble the Kah-Gash, but we hoped to capture the pieces and hold them from the Demonata forever. We learnt to influence the pieces, but only as the Demonata did. We can keep them in place a while, but eventually they slip free."

"Is that the same when the demons capture them?" I ask.

"Yes."

"Then why worry?" I shrug. "If they can't hold on

to a piece forever, they can't collect them all, can they?"

"Unfortunately, yes," Raz says. "Sometimes all three pieces exist in a universe at the same time, as they do now. When I say we can't hold on to a piece for long, I mean tens of thousands of years. That's more than enough time for the Demonata to unite the parts. All they need is a lucky break.

"So we continued to fight," Raz says wearily. "Every time they captured a piece, we set it free. It could have gone on like that until the end of time, except there were casualties. Some of us always died when we raided. A few here, a few there. When you add them up over millions, then billions of years..." He shudders.

"We're not afraid of death," Raz says. "But we couldn't continue that way indefinitely, because–"

"–you can't have children," I interrupt, beating him to the punch.

"Correct." He smiles sadly. "At some point we would become extinct. Then the demons would be free to track down the pieces of the Kah-Gash and restore the original universe, only this time it would be exclusively theirs.

"We couldn't accept such a fate, so we did something we were never meant to. We played God and interfered with the creatures of the new universe.

We've been paying for that mistake ever since. And the universe has been paying for it too."

Raz turns his face away and says with shame, "We're the reason the Demonata can cross from their universe to ours." He brushes a hand across his cheeks, and though I can't be certain, I think the Old Creature is wiping away guilty tears.

# WORLD OF THE DEAD

→We return to the room with the garden and Raz constucts a new window. We travel for a long time through the sub-universe of lights, finally emerging on top of a stone slab. The walls of this chamber are dotted with holes and windows, through which I can see thousands of tombs and monuments, encircling us like silent, frozen sentries.

Raz slips through one of the larger holes and I follow, gazing solemnly at the ranks of graves. Even though the tombs differ in style and size to those on Earth, there's no doubt that this is a graveyard. It has the feel of death.

"This place is massive," I whisper, goosebumps rising.

"It is a cemetery world," Raz says.

"You mean everybody's dead?" I gulp. "Was it a war?"

"There was never life on this planet," Raz says. "But there are populated planets nearby and advanced beings move freely between them. For centuries they have been bringing their dead here, laying them to rest on a world of their own."

A world of the dead. My goosebumps spread. I'm not easily spooked, but this is creeping me out big time.

"By shaping the minds of this universe's creatures, we hoped to cheat destiny," Raz says softly, returning to his lecture. "We knew we would die before the universe ended. We thought if we spread intelligence, the beings we created might carry on the fight.

"There are now millions of races with the power of thought. Many are more advanced than your people. But intelligence was never intended for this universe. The earliest creatures showed no signs of evolving and developing souls."

"What do you mean by that?" I stop him.

"Every intelligent being has a soul," Raz says. "Animals don't. A soul forms when a creature thinks for the first time, when it reasons and makes plans. It is a fascinating process. In some species it happens in every member at the same moment. In most, one of them makes a mental leap, then bears young and they pass it on, intelligence spreading like a disease.

"We cultivated the *disease*. It was much harder than we imagined, but once we made the breakthrough, we quickly mastered the arts of education, then split into small groups and set off for the far reaches of the universe, sowing intelligence everywhere we went.

"We had no right to disturb the natural balance," Raz sighs. "But *you* are a child of our meddling. Would you rather exist as a mindless beast, running wild, no understanding of the past or plans for the future?"

"No," I answer after a short pause.

"Nor do most others. They *have* the choice. We can't force a species to evolve. Some fight it and return to their simpler ways. But most rise to the challenges we set. Life is easier for animals, but so much richer for those with the ability to love and hate, fight and make peace, dream and hope."

Raz falls silent as we walk among the tombs and headstones. After a while I come to a small, unimpressive tomb. I almost walk past, but Raz coughs softly and points towards the upper right corner.

A tiny chess board has been carved into it. As my eyes narrow, Raz points to the left corner, where another board has been carved. Then he nods at a tomb four rows over. A large, intricate board has been painted over the centre of this one, the name of the deceased worked in among the black and white squares.

"The Boards are key to the process," Raz says. "We created them out of material drawn from the Crux.

Modelling them after the Kah-Gash, we created mini-universes of sixty-four zones. Once a species evolves to a certain point, we isolate their souls and take them into a Board, so that they can develop at an accelerated rate. We also teach them about the origins of the universe, the Kah-Gash and the Demonata, the need to reach for the stars, to fight for the future of the universe."

"How come I don't know all that?" I ask.

"You have an undeveloped brain," Raz says, then raises his hands as I bristle. "I mean humans in general. You have not evolved to the point where you can make sense of all that we taught you. Every species is the same. It takes time to work your way through the mysteries of life." Raz grimaces. "Humans will never complete that journey. The Demonata will cut short their growth. Universal understanding is not to be yours."

I blink and look away, stomach tightening. I spot something far overhead. I think it's a falling star, but as I focus, I realise it's a spaceship. Unlike the floating city, this looks more like the rockets I've seen in movies and on the covers of science-fiction books.

"A glorified hearse," Raz says.

We watch in silence until the ship settles out of sight beyond the ranks of tombs. "Can we go and see the burial?" I ask.

"No," Raz says. "I have something else to show you." He leads me through a maze until we come to a black, round stone. Its edges are as smooth as a polished gem's. It's set in a small pit, circled by a number of large tombs. Candles burn around the edges of the pit, but they're not normal candles — the wick doesn't burn down and the flames never flicker in the soft wind.

There's a magical buzz coming from the stone. My fingers curl inwards and my nostrils widen. Magic floods my pores.

"It's another lodestone," I note.

"Yes," Raz says. "Beranabus thought the stones were of our making, but they are actually the remains of planets from the original universe. Most were reduced to dust, but fragments of some survived and drifted through space, sometimes burying themselves in the fabric of freshly forming worlds.

"The stones were charged with the magic of the original universe. We used them to travel swiftly from one planet to another. They acted as universal markers, guiding us, allowing us to cross vast expanses of space swiftly. Unfortunately the lodestones could be used to serve the forces of evil as well." Raz laughs bitterly. "We never guessed that the species we assisted might prove as vicious as the demons we hoped they would fight."

"Mages used lodestones to open windows to the Demonata universe," I groan.

"We assumed this universe's creatures would care primarily for their own," Raz says. "But many craved power. Each world produced individuals with magical talent. Most used their power to do good, but some became tyrants. They crushed their enemies and ruled with a monstrous authority."

"You could have stopped them," I growl.

"And replaced them?" Raz asks wryly. "Established our favourites as rulers? No. We were determined to guide, not rule. We looked on with despair as the rotten few caused misery for millions. But we never intervened. Every species must be free to make their mistakes, enjoy their triumphs, lament their catastrophes. That is our fundamental belief."

Raz sighs again. "The windows were bad enough, but then some used more powerful lodestones to create tunnels and entire civilisations fell. We realised more would follow, that the Demonata would cross in greater numbers and spread. We thought about shutting the project down." He chuckles humourlessly.

"Why didn't you?" I frown.

Raz shakes his head. "You don't realise what that would have entailed. We had visited millions of worlds. There were billions of intelligent beings scattered through the universe. We'd have had to–"

"–kill them all," I finish hoarsely.

Raz nods. "That was not an option, so we dismissed it. Besides, the demons could not ruin *every* world or kill *every* living being. It was physically impossible. The Demonata might destroy much, but not all. Life would continue, even when we were gone.

"That changed sixteen hundred years ago." Raz's features darken. "We had pressed on with the programme. All looked positive. But then, on your world, an insignificant, unremarkable girl altered everything. She turned the laws of life on their head, and introduced a new player to the game, one who could guarantee victory for the Demonata."

I gulp. "You're talking about Bec, aren't you?"

"Yes," Raz says angrily.

"And the new player?" I ask.

He stares at me heavily, then says, "*Death*."

# THE REAPER UNLEASHED

→"What are you talking about?" I mutter. "According to Art, death always existed, even in the original universe."

"As a force," Raz says. "Death was like time or gravity. It was simply a thing that happened. Bec changed that. First she stole a piece of the Kah-Gash from Lord Loss. Then–"

"From Lord Loss?" I interrupt, startled. "Art said the pieces never turned up in demons who were alive before the Big Bang."

"They don't," Raz says.

"Then Lord Loss isn't one of the major demons?" I whisper. The demon master is by far the most powerful foe I've ever faced. If there are others even stronger than him…

"There are many greater than he is," Raz says gloomily, "but he has a unique power. The piece of the Kah-Gash nestled within him for thousands of years. That's why he alone of the masters is able to cross freely between universes.

"When Bec unconsciously stole Lord Loss's piece of the Kah-Gash, it was cause for wonder — that had never happened before. But then she did something even more incredible. When Lord Loss killed her, her soul remained.

"Death has always meant the end. When a body dies, the soul moves on, maybe to another realm, maybe to be reincarnated, maybe to nothingness — we can only guess. But no soul ever cheated death."

"Bec was just a ghost," I mutter. "Ghosts are nothing new."

"Ghosts are shadows of the living," Raz says. "They're after-images of people, like the temporary glow a light leaves when it's quenched. Bec was different. She was fully conscious, memories intact, a complete spirit."

I shrug. "She's part of the Kah-Gash. She used her power to stay, just as Lord Loss used it to cross universes. What's the big deal?"

"Death was an absolute," Raz snaps. "The Kah-Gash had no control over it. All beings had to answer death's summons. Until Bec."

The rocket we saw touch down rises with a roar that shakes the tombs around me. I think the structures are going to shatter, but as the rocket parts the clouds and powers away from the planet, they settle down again.

"We don't know how Bec cheated death," Raz says softly. "We're not sure if she chose to remain, or if the Kah-Gash kept her, aware of the side-effects."

"What side-effects?"

Raz is silent a moment. Then he moves away from the lodestone, through the tombs, back to the chamber. As I follow, he speaks.

"Death was a force, but when Bec defied it, that force developed a mind. It became aware of itself, the universes, its role. And unfortunately it reacted with anger."

"This is madness," I grumble. "Death's not a person. It can't *react*."

"It can now," Raz disagrees. "It constructed a body. Prior to Bec, beings died and souls passed on. But the new Death has the power to harness souls. It can deny them passage to whatever lies beyond. It built a huge, shadowy body out of–"

"*The Shadow!*" I cry, coming to a standstill, eyes widening with horror.

I'm trembling. It all makes horrible sense now. Beranabus was right — the Shadow *is* the greatest threat we've ever faced. Only it's far worse than he imagined. You can't cheat death and you can't hide from it.

"Precisely," Raz sighs. "Since death claims all things, Death knows where all things are. The body of Death can only thrive in an area of magic, so it resides in the demon universe. But its reach extends to all worlds. It can guide the Demonata to wherever there is life."

"But why is it working for them?" I moan.

Raz makes a humming noise. "This is speculation, but we believe the Demonata and Death share a common goal — the restoration of the Kah-Gash. If they achieve it, the life forms of this universe will cease to exist. The Demonata will return to their immortal ways. The Old Creatures will drift along sadly. And Death's task will be vastly lessened."

"What task?" I frown.

"The harvesting of souls. Death's job is far harder now than it was before the Big Bang — so many souls to process. It seems to think the job is *too* hard, and is working to – as you humans would aptly put it – lighten its workload."

"We have to stop it," I gasp. "We have to find the Shadow and destroy it. If Death has a body, it can be attacked. If we kill it, maybe its mind will unravel."

"We do not think it is possible to kill Death," Raz murmurs. "It will simply put another body together. There will never be a shortage of souls."

"The Kah-Gash," I snap. "We can use that."

Raz pulls a face. "The Kah-Gash never had power over death. Also, as I said, it might have worked through Bec to grant Death consciousness in the first place. The Kah-Gash has changed. In the past, the pieces cut random paths through the universes. But since Bec defied death, the other parts have worked their way to your planet. They both cropped up there shortly after she died. We could do nothing about Bec's piece – she was beyond our grasp – but we directed the other pair into forms of our choosing and sent them far away.

"They escaped and returned to Earth, in Grubitsch Grady and you."

"You think the Kah-Gash wants to reunite?" I frown.

"It looks that way. Perhaps the Kah-Gash wishes to fight Death, to preserve the universes. Or maybe it too yearns for a return to simpler ways, and is using Death to achieve its goal. We don't know. We can only fear."

"I guess there's only one way to find out," I grunt. "We have to go back. I'll join with Bec and Grubbs, try to control the Kah-Gash, and hope for the best. There's no other way, is there?"

"Actually," Raz coughs, "there is. But you're not going to like it..."

# NOAH MK II

→When we cross to the next world, I find myself on a large, circular, metallic platform. It's covered by a domed glass roof. There are banks of sophisticated-looking computers running along the sides.

"Not so sophisticated really," Raz murmurs. "This was designed as a viewing station by one of the lesser species. We could have arranged a more advanced craft, but they like to do things themselves. Look down."

I nudge to the edge, not sure what to expect. As I approach, panels of glass slide back and a telescope revolves into place before me.

A world like Earth lies a few miles below. There are massive buildings, wide roads, parks and ponds. Some of the buildings have glass roofs or are open topped. I can see all sorts of creatures moving around inside them, a bewildering variety of animals, birds, lizards and more, many defying description.

"It looks like a zoo," I remark.

"It is," Raz says. "But all of them have souls and are here of their own choice. They know of the Demonata and the threat this universe faces, and have pledged themselves to our cause."

The air hums with magic. As I cast my gaze around, I spot lodestones dotted everywhere, of all shapes and sizes.

"It's an ark," Raz says. "You know the biblical story of the ark, how Noah took in a pair of every species and spared them from the flood."

"Was that real?" I ask.

"It doesn't matter." He waves the question away. "*Our* ark is real, and we have to deal with far worse than a flood. This is why you're here, why we've shown you all that you've seen and revealed so much."

"I don't get it. You want me to live here?"

Raz laughs. "We'd have brought you here directly if that was the case, telling you only as much as you needed to know, as we did with the others. There are already humans on this ark. Your people are not among the more advanced, but we brought some here anyway, for *you*."

"I'm still lost," I mutter.

"We want you to be the new Noah," Raz says. "We want you to protect these creatures and guide them, evading the Demonata and Death, always remaining one step ahead of those who would destroy them. We want you to save the universe."

It sounds ridiculous. I'm tempted to laugh. Except I know Raz isn't joking.

"How?" I whisper.

"We've planted scores of lodestones across this planet," Raz says. "Enough to last an eternity. This is a world of never-ending magical energy. We designed it to be a haven, a warship, a nursery. Food will always be abundant. Species will never struggle with infertility. Magicians will be born to every generation."

"You're going to make a last stand here?" I frown. "This is a fortress?"

"No fortress could stand against our enemies," Raz says. "If this world was a thousand times more powerful than it is, it still wouldn't hold long against a mass demon attack. The Demonata don't know about the ark yet, but they'll discover it eventually and come. When they arrive, it must not be here."

"Huh?" I gawp.

"We will ensure they never open a tunnel to this world, by guarding each stone zealously. With no direct route of attack, Death will lead them to nearby planets and they'll launch armies from there. When that happens… when the net is closing and the end looks certain… it will be *your* time."

"What am I supposed to do?" I scowl. "Hold up a STOP sign?"

"You will open a window and slip away to another part of the universe," Raz says. "And you'll take the planet with you."

He says it so simply that at first I nod as if it's no big thing. Then it hits me and I turn from the edge of the platform and stare incredulously.

"Take the *planet* with me?" I repeat stupidly.

"When you've opened windows before, others have been able to slip through. This will be similar, only you'll have to open a bigger window."

"You're insane!" I yelp. "I've never opened a window more then seven or eight feet tall."

"That's because you never needed a larger window," Raz says calmly. "You can do far more than you've demanded of yourself. With our guidance you'll learn to open a larger window and curve it, so it surrounds the world. That way, rather than propel the world through the window, it can close around the planet."

I stare at Raz wordlessly. I don't know what to think.

"Think of victory," Raz growls. "Think of life. Think of the demons you'll defy, the doom you'll spare everyone here."

"It's impossible..."

"No," Raz insists. "It *can* work. That's no guarantee that it *will* – there might be obstacles ahead which we can't predict – but we believe in the plan."

My mind's whirling. "But when I die, my piece of the Kah-Gash will link up with the others. You've already said you can't control it."

Raz clears his throat. "That brings us to the part you're not going to like. As you say, we won't be able to harness your piece of the Kah-Gash when you die, so we need to find a way around that. Kernel, what would you think if we asked you to make the ultimate sacrifice for the sake of the universe?"

"You want me to kill myself?" I ask with surprising calmness.

"No." Raz leans forward, eyes sparkling. "We want you to live forever!"

# A WARNING

→We spend the night wandering the ark, sharing food and drink with some of the many creatures aboard. They don't know who I am or the special task Raz has asked of me. They think I'm just another face in the crowd.

I'm surprised, as I talk with the sometimes multi-limbed, multi-headed, multicoloured aliens, by how alike we are. Not in looks, clothes or customs. But they have the same concepts of good and evil. Family is important to them. Most are religious. They have dreams and hopes for the future.

"Are all civilisations like this?" I ask Raz as we stroll beneath trees full of bat-like beings. A few are playing a game on a chess board.

"No," Raz says. "We chose from the more compassionate species. They have a fighting spirit – we need warriors – but they can control their tempers. This world has to last an eternity. We cannot tolerate internal conflict."

"It might happen anyway," I note, watching a couple of bats chase each other through the branches, squealing happily. "People change, so I guess this lot do too. You can't know what they'll be like in a million years. Groups might splinter. War could erupt."

"Perhaps." Raz sighs. "We'll use magic to preserve the balance as best we can. Evolution will be curbed, so there'll be no physical changes, but we can't take all possibilities into consideration. We'll plan as far ahead as possible. After that... As you would say, it's in the lap of the gods."

I still haven't reached a decision. I'm weighing up all that the universe stands to gain against all that I will personally lose.

They want me to become a living tunnel between universes. Sometimes a mage becomes part of a tunnel and lives as long as the tunnel remains open. They don't age or die. If I agree to this, I'll live until the end of time. Death won't be able to claim me. I can keep moving the ark around, protecting this small pocket of survivors while all others are tracked down by the Demonata and slaughtered.

It's not foolproof. My piece of the Kah-Gash might desert me when it realises what I'm doing, or Death might find a way to trap the ark. But the Old Creatures think it will work. *If* I play along.

In their position, I'd force the guy with the power

to accept. I wouldn't give him any say in the matter. I'd open a tunnel, make him part of it and leave him with no option but to do what was necessary.

But the Old Creatures believe I have the right to choose. It's the creed they live by. They'll guide their foster children in the right direction, but they won't force us. Ever. Even if the fate of the universe is at stake.

It's not a nice future – I don't want to spend the rest of eternity as a cog in a machine – but if I refuse to cooperate and everything falls to the demon hordes, there won't be any kind of a future at all. The Demonata will either get their hands on all three pieces of the Kah-Gash and destroy everything immediately. Or they'll work their way through the universe, world by world, and gradually grind us into dust. Either way, universal catastrophe.

But if I stay, I'll be surrendering all but a slim fraction of this universe to the demons. I might keep the millions on this world alive, but trillions of others will perish horribly. If I go back and link up with Bec and Grubbs… if we reassemble the Kah-Gash and test it against Death… then the universe has a chance. It might even be possible to save Earth.

Is it better to make a stand, fail and lose all, or sacrifice unimaginable numbers of lives in order to keep a select handful alive? I don't know! This task should have fallen to someone equipped to meet it, like Beranabus. He'd have said yes to the Old Creatures in an instant, without batting an eyelid.

"Perhaps that's why he wasn't chosen," Raz murmurs. "We don't know why the Kah-Gash selects those it inhabits. It might be random, or it might be the work of a higher force. Maybe the universe chose someone who would weigh both sides equally, who wasn't so certain of his path that he'd ignore all others."

"But what if I make the wrong choice?" I groan.

"You can only do what you believe is right," Raz says. "Consider the angles. Heed your instinct. Decide. If you are wrong, at least you will have been true to yourself. Life asks questions of us all. We don't always know the answers. Most times we have to guess."

"But you think I should stay," I press, trying to force Raz to decide for me.

"Yes," Raz says. "But we also believed we were acting in the universe's best interests when we encouraged evolution. We are not always right."

I nod glumly. We've passed from beneath the trees and I can see the sky again. There are several moons, smaller than Earth's, different colours. They look like huge marbles. Thinking of marbles, I remember when Art was stolen by a monster from another world. I darted through a window of light to try and rescue him. I didn't know what lay on the other side. The safe option would have been to wait and consider my actions. But then the window would have closed, Art would have been lost. I'd have regretted my indecision for the rest of my life.

Raz squints at me. "You are going back," he notes with surprise.

"Maybe Death can't be defeated," I sigh. "Maybe the Demonata have won and this ark is all we can hope to protect. But I have to *try* to stop them. If I run now, I'll always wonder if there wasn't something I could have done to save *everyone*.

"If I fight Death and fail, I'll return to do what you wish, assuming I survive. But if I quit now, it'll gnaw away at me... at my soul... forever."

I lower my gaze and wipe tears from my eyes. I don't know when I started crying, but my cheeks are soaked. "Open a window," I croak. "I'm going home."

→The journey back passes unremarkably. A series of lights, windows and worlds. We follow a different route most of the way, but the chambers we pass through are much the same. I don't explore any of the worlds. I'm fully focused on the battle to come, the huge risk I'm taking, what will happen if I fail. I wish I could be positive about my decision, but I'm full of doubts. I think about changing my mind at least ten times an hour.

Eventually we start passing through worlds I remember from the trip out. I get excited as we draw closer to Earth. I might be going to my death, but if that's to be my destiny, at least I'll die on home soil.

Finally, as my stomach's starting to rumble again, we hit Atlantis and come to a stop. Raz looks around to make sure there are no giant slugs, then glances at me. "I'll wait here for you."

I'm surprised. "You're not coming with me?"

"No. I will escort you back, but I won't cross with you. You must face Death by yourself, as everyone must when their time comes. If you wish to return, you can find me here."

"But I can't operate the smaller lights," I remind him.

"You won't need to," Raz says. "You will be able to use the normal lights to search for me. It will take a long time to piece them together – at least several hours – but just think of me and you will find the way."

"How will I breathe while crossing?" I ask.

Raz goes to one of the lodestones and cuts off a sliver of rock with a fingernail, as easily as slicing through paper. "Put this in your pocket," he says, handing it to me. "Draw on its power if you come back. It will sustain you."

"You're sure?" I ask, eyeing the tiny chip of rock suspiciously.

"Yes."

"How long will you wait?" I ask.

"As long as it takes," he says. "I will know when you are… finished."

"You mean when I'm dead," I smile.

"If the hand plays out that way, yes. But I hope it doesn't."

Raz sets to work on the window and it materialises minutes later. I start to tremble and my stomach clenches. I was never the bravest. I hate fighting. But when I have to, I do. Wincing, I step forward.

"One last thing," Raz stops me, then hesitates. "This is a delicate matter. I don't wish to cast doubts without proof, but it's important that you know about the possibility of the threat."

"What threat?" I grunt.

"The girl," Raz says softly. "Her piece of the Kah-Gash was originally part of Lord Loss."

"So?" I ask warily.

"It was in the demon master for a long time. Pieces normally merge with beings who live no more than a few hundred years. They're influenced by those they share a life with. Having been part of Lord Loss for so long, her piece might have been more affected by the demon than by other hosts."

"Are you saying…?" I stop, the thought unfinished, not wanting to continue.

"The Kah-Gash could be manipulating the girl," Raz says. "Perhaps it spared her soul in order to give Death its freedom. Maybe it wants to restore the original universe. Bec is of good heart, but the best of people can be tricked and misused.

"We might be worrying unnecessarily," Raz concludes. "You may have nothing to fear. But watch her, Kernel. Use those sharp eyes of yours. Look for treachery and be prepared for it. *Beware the priestess, Bec.*"

# WELCOME HOME

→Raz leads me through the sub-universe of lights for the last time, then bids me a quick farewell and propels me forward. Before I can yell goodbye, I'm thrust through a window and straight into the middle of a nightmarish war. No time to gather my senses. I have to adapt immediately or die.

I'm in the middle of a city. Blood and corpses everywhere. The air's thick with the scent of demons, and also with the buzz of magic, which I swiftly tap into. I try to erect a shield around myself, but something clatters into me before I can complete it. A beast rolls with me to the ground and comes up spitting. It's a wolfish creature, long fangs, claws the size of butchers' knives, hot yellow eyes. It turns, faces me, snarls — then leaps.

I raise my hands to repel the monster, but instead of attacking me, it jumps over my head and tears into something behind, howling with bloodthirsty delight. Whirling, I spot the wolfish beast battling a demon.

The wolf rips at the demon's ribcage, fangs snapping in search of guts.

Wary and confused, I cast my gaze around. There are more wolfen animals on the street and they're all fighting demons. Soldiers are at work too, tackling the demonic invaders, showering them with bullets. They can't kill the Demonata but they can injure, disrupt and stall them.

There's a burst of magic to my right. I spot a small girl rounding on a demon, frying it with magic until its head explodes and its brains splatter the wall behind it. I'm so pleased to see a familiar face, I forget all about Raz's warning and call enthusiastically, "Bec!"

She looks up. Her eyes widen with shock, then her lips spread into a smile. She yells something, but as she does, one of the wolf-like beasts wraps its arms around me and howls into my ear, obscuring all other sounds.

I lash at the creature, trying to wriggle free, gathering my energy to fight back. Before I can, the beast laughs and says, "Surely you recognise me."

I place the voice instantly, but can't believe it. I stare at the creature. He's two or three feet taller than when I last saw him, and his face is warped — dark skin, lots of blood vessels, tufts of wiry ginger hair, a yellow tinge to his eyes, mouth bigger, teeth sharper. His body is lacerated with cuts and bruises. But it's definitely–

"*Grubbs!*" I roar. "What the hell's happened? You look like a werewolf."

"I am," he chuckles. "That's my pack." He waves a hairy hand at the wolves. His fingers are twisted and bulging, the nails more like claws. He could probably pop my head one-handed.

"But... how... what...?"

"I'll deal with this lot first and explain later," he growls, tugging at the waist of his trousers. They only just fit him. He's naked otherwise, chest exposed, rippling with muscles. He's stained with blood — different colours, so I know it's demon blood, not his own. Some of the stains are fresh, dripping from his skin and soaking into his hair. But others are caked in. He's been in the wars since we parted, and he looks like he's been loving every moment.

As Grubbs pounds away to attack a group of vicious demons, I put my questions on hold and focus on how best I can help. It's a dirty, messy battle. Normally demons cross singly or in small groups. But there are dozens running riot here. This is no ordinary crossing. It's the work of a powerful, organised, intelligent foe.

As the battle rages around me, I complete my shield, then focus on the patches of light in the air. A quick check reveals two windows set a few hundred feet from each other. Demons are pouring through both. That suits me perfectly. I might not be a great fighter, but I can turn the tide of this battle single-handed.

Picking a path through the warring forces, I hurry to the nearest window. It's a large pink panel. Ignoring the demons spilling out of it, protected by my shield, I thrust my hands into the centre of the panel and pull at the patches. Within seconds the window pulses, tears apart, then snaps out of existence.

The demons closest to me become alert to the threat I pose. If I can shut down the second window they'll be stranded and demons can't survive long on this world. Screeching for support, they hurl themselves at me. For a split-second I think I'm doomed. But then the road explodes at my feet, scattering the converging demons. As they scream, blinded and injured by the flying debris, sheets of fire drop on them from the air, setting them ablaze, sending them thrashing away madly.

I look for my saviour and find two angels, Bec and Meera Flame, standing side by side, hands raised, energy flowing through them, wreaking havoc. Meera's always been a stunner, but she looks more beautiful than ever now, and Bec is no strain on the eyes either. Having said that, I'd probably think anyone who saved my life was gorgeous — even Grubbs!

"Come with me!" I yell at them and press towards the second window. Meera and Bec back me up, blasting the demons ahead of me, calling for support from the soldiers and werewolves.

The smarter demons realise they're fighting a lost cause. Cursing foully, they dash through the window to the safety of their own universe, driving back those who were trying to cross. More break for the window, but get tangled up with each other or waylaid by our forces. Panic sets it. The street echoes with the hysterical wails of monsters who know they don't have long to live.

A minute later I'm ripping apart the window, and once it dissolves the demons are finished. As magic drains from the air, some of the weaker specimens collapse and rot. The others battle on hatefully, wanting to kill more humans before they die. But it's hopeless. The bullets from the soldiers' guns rip them to shreds, and without the aid of magic they have no way of putting their forms back together. They're torn to pieces. Soon only humans and werewolves are standing. We laugh and cheer, punch the air with fists, then hurry to embrace one another. We might be standing ankle-deep in rancid guts, blood and other vile juices, surrounded by corpses, but we're standing victorious — and that feels *good!*

→Grubbs wants to press on as soon as the danger's been averted. The Demonata and their twisted, human mages have been working flat out, crossing in waves. This is the fifth city Grubbs and Bec have defended in less than three days. And they've already received word of a planned sixth crossing. Grubbs is eager to get there as swiftly as possible, to stop the mage if he can, or prepare for the demons if not.

"Do you know when the window will open?" I ask.

"Within the next thirty-six hours."

"No sooner than a day?"

"No."

"Then what's the rush?"

"It's on the other side of the globe," he growls. "By the time we get to the airport, load everyone up, make the flight, roll off at the other end..."

"You don't have to do that any more," I tut. "I'll open a window and we can be there in a matter of minutes."

"Oh. I forgot." He squints. "But the mage..."

"As soon as we get there, I'll locate the forming window and we'll put a stop to it. Let's rest a while. You lot look beat. We can afford to take a day off now that *I'm* back on the scene."

"Show-off," Grubbs grunts, but he can't hide a grin.

Teams move in to clean up. I was expecting hysteria, crowds of terrified onlookers, confusion and chaos. But it all runs smoothly. Grubbs explains that the world has woken up to the existence of demons. They've attacked five densely populated cities in swift succession. Even though they've been driven off each time, thousands have been killed, cities torn apart, in full view of camera crews.

The Disciples kept the war with the Demonata quiet for a long time, with highly placed allies in most of the major news agencies and governments. But it's no longer possible to cover up. The world knows about demons now, and while panic has swept the globe, most people are behaving sensibly and heeding the advice of the Disciples. They're evacuating targeted cities quickly and calmly, or staying indoors if they can't get out in time. Volunteers have flocked to recruiting centres — Disciples test for mages each time a window opens. Those with no magical ability are working with soldiers, doctors and nurses, street cleaners, electricians, plumbers... rallying to the call, doing all they can to restore order and sweep up after an attack so that life can continue as normal.

While Grubbs gathers his pack of werewolves – there were thirty-seven to start with, but only sixteen remain – and takes them off to their holding pens, I retire to a deserted hotel with Bec, Meera and a guy in a tattered stage-magician's outfit. It's ripped all over, revealing more than it conceals, and is caked with dirt and blood. But he wears it with pride, knotting the strips of cloth around himself. His fingers (two on his left hand are missing) tremble as he ties the knots. He looks like a man who's only just holding himself together.

A frightened manager – but one who stayed when all else fled – shows us up to the hotel's finest suite. He treats us like celebrities, takes our orders, promises to do his best to process them promptly, and leaves us to collapse into chairs (Meera claims the bed) and stare at each other in weary silence.

"This is Kirilli Kovacs," Bec finally says, introducing me to the guy in the magician's costume. "He's a Disciple."

Kirilli waves weakly. Blood is seeping through the bandage around the two missing fingers on his left hand, and also through the many bandages wrapped around his body. Bec sighs, rises and limps across the room. She sets to work on healing the worst of Kirilli's wounds, drawing on the traces of magic that remain in the air. He studies her blankly while she works, like a child being cleaned by its mother.

"Where have you been?" Meera asks, then snaps her fingers at me before I can reply. "No. Let's eat, grab some sleep and wait for Grubbs. We've got loads to tell you and I guess you've got lots to tell us too."

"More than you could ever imagine," I mutter.

"Will it save for a few hours?" she asks and I shrug.

"Great." Then, forgetting about the food, she drops back, shuts her eyes and is snoring softly a minute later.

→Grubbs joins us as the food's being wheeled in. He tucks into Meera's meal – nobody wants to wake her – and asks the manager to deliver more food in nine hours. Then we retreat to different corners of the suite and make ourselves comfortable. I use magic to help me sleep.

We rise nine hours later and feast on the waiting meal. Meera's especially ravenous. I thought Grubbs was a big eater, but she beats him hollow and is still chewing at strips of chicken long after the rest of us have set our plates aside.

We swap tales while we eat, and the stories continue long after we've finished munching. Grubbs and Meera tell me all that happened once he left us at the hospital. With Shark and a squad of soldiers, they went in pursuit of Prae Athim, the head of the Lambs, and tracked her to the appropriately named Wolf Island. A load of Grubbs's cousins had been genetically modified and bred, producing hundreds of savage, wolfen offspring. They were waiting for the trio on the island.

Juni Swan was also waiting. She drove them back and left them at the mercy of the werewolves. The plan was to get her hands on Grubbs's piece of the Kah-Gash and deliver it to her new master. The simplest way was to let the werewolves butcher him, then direct the piece into a form of her choosing when it soared free.

They'd have all perished, but Grubbs unleashed the werewolf within himself and took command of his hairy relatives. He turned the tables on their foes, and although Juni escaped, they killed her conspirators.

Grubbs is sullen when he describes his fight with Juni. He doesn't look anyone in the eye. He's clearly hiding something from us, but I've no idea what.

Twelve of them hit the island. Prae Athim made it thirteen. But only Grubbs, Meera, Shark and someone called Timas Brauss made it off, leaving Prae behind to look after the werewolves, except for the thirty-seven Grubbs brought with him — his own personal army.

"That's pretty much it," he grunts. "Shark's out of action for a while. Timas is busy elsewhere, looking in on Shark whenever he can. Meera and I linked up with Dervish, Bec and Kirilli, and we've been fighting demons ever since."

"Where is Dervish?" I ask, anticipating the worst. "Is he..."

"...dead?" Grubbs snorts. "Hardly. I wanted to send him back to the demon universe – he'd live longer there – but he wants to stay and fight till he drops. He stood by us in the first two battles, but he was wrecked afterwards. Now he's acting as a talent-spotting scout. He's on the edge of this city with thousands of people. When the window opened, he tested them for magical ability. He's come up with some decent mages at the last two stops. I hope he finds more this time. We could use them — I'm running out of werewolves."

Nobody seems bothered by Grubbs's appearance. He looks like something out of a horror movie, twisted and misshapen, picking bits of flesh from between his teeth and under his fingernails. But they're all treating him as if nothing's changed. I guess, in times as deadly as these, you can't worry too much about the looks of those who stand beside you.

But I don't like it. He's not just physically different. Something's changed inside him too. He's rougher than before, more accepting of violence and death. He reminds me of Beranabus, the way he callously wrote off human casualties, like he wasn't truly one of us. Raz told me to watch out for Bec, but I think Grubbs is the one I need to worry about.

I ask how Beranabus died. Bec answers, telling her story swiftly. They found Kirilli on the ship after they left me, then descended to the hold, where Juni was waiting. She used a lodestone to open a strange window, through which the Shadow crossed. As Bec fought it, she absorbed some of its memories and realised it was Death. She informed Beranabus and he sent them packing, staying behind to fight their shadowy foe and buy them time.

"He transformed," she whispers. "He let his demonic half take over. I think he meant to die, whether he won or lost. He wasn't sure he could change back once he set the demon free."

"Nobody can ever change back," Grubbs rumbles, scratching a cut on his chest, then licking flaky blood from his fingers.

Beranabus destroyed the lodestone, sending Death back to the universe of the Demonata. But the shadowy creature struck before it was whipped away, and the ancient magician died in the hold, to be swallowed by the sea.

Bec, Dervish, Kirilli and Sharmila made it back to the deck, fighting their way through an army of zombies. But they were trapped there, imprisoned by a barrier of magical energy as the ship sank.

"Sharmila sacrificed herself to save the rest of us," Bec says miserably. "She lay against the barrier and we exploded her, punching a hole through to safety." She stops, tears welling in her eyes.

"It should have been me," Kirilli says. He hasn't said much so far. Now when he speaks he keeps his head low, embarrassed. "I was the weakest. I ran when the others fought. I've served the Disciples well in a non-combative capacity, but I'm no hero. She should be here now, not me."

"You got that right," someone laughs and when I look round I find Dervish standing behind me, smiling weakly. He looks even older than he did on the ship, frail, trembling, about two steps away from death. The six silver, purple-tipped spikes he grew on his head in the oasis are as impressive as ever, but apart from that he looks like a man on his last legs.

"Good to see you, old-timer," I grin.

"You too," he says. "We thought you were zombie pâté." He winks at Kirilli, who's glowering. "Modesty doesn't become you, Kovacs. I prefer you when you're blowing hot air and claiming credit for every kill in a five-kilometre radius."

"I claim nothing from any man," Kirilli snarls.

Dervish chuckles, then says, "What have I missed?"

"We've been bringing Kernel up to date," Grubbs yawns, as if the stories of their adventures bore him. "Now he's about to return the favour."

Nodding reluctantly, not sure how to begin, I cast my mind back to when the dead first stirred on the ship, take a quick breath and launch myself at it.

# RESTLESS SOULS

→I speak clearly and concisely. I don't think I miss anything important, though I have to backtrack a few times when I recall bits that I overlooked. The others listen in silence, their faces lengthening as I reveal the direness of our situation, the belief of the Old Creatures that the universe is doomed.

There's silence when I finish. Everyone's brooding. Even Grubbs looks troubled — his face has altered and become more human.

"I wouldn't have returned," Dervish finally says. "I've faced a lot in my time, stepped up to all sorts of challenges. But in your position, I'd have stayed on the ark. I wouldn't have had the guts to come back with so much at risk. I'd have gone with the safe option."

"Coward," Kirilli laughs.

"I don't like being the practical one," Meera mutters, "but what if he imagined it all? Travelling to the centre of the universe… life starting with a chess board… aliens nudging us up the evolutionary ladder… an ark world. That's pretty far-fetched, even by our standards. What if he's crazy? No offence, Kernel."

"None taken." I sigh. "I wish it *was* my imagination. But I'm sure it wasn't."

"The Kah-Gash told me I was the trigger," Grubbs says slowly, and he has that shifty look in his eyes again. "In the hospital, when the three of us were together, it said I had the power to unite and direct it. So that part of the story's true."

"It's all true," Bec snaps. "Let's not waste time pretending otherwise. Our world is doomed. The universe is damned. Unless we defeat Death."

"No one ever cheats death," Dervish says.

"I did," Bec reminds him.

I said nothing of Raz's suspicions about Bec. We need to work together, not abandon ourselves to paranoia.

"We need a plan," Meera says. "Mr Trigger Man — any ideas?"

Grubbs shrugs. "Track Death down and rip it to pieces. Easy."

"You almost sound like you believe that," Dervish snorts.

"I do," Grubbs insists. "Death made a mistake when it took a body. That puts it on a par with us. From what you told me, Beranabus gave as good as he got when he went up against the Shadow. He sent it screaming back to the foul realm of the Demonata. We're stronger than Beranabus. We can inflict more damage. I say we reassemble the Kah-Gash, hit Death hard and end this."

"I don't know," Bec murmurs. "The Kah-Gash frightens me more than Death or the Demonata. They can only kill us, but the Kah-Gash can wipe out the universe, so we never even existed in the first place. I don't think we should unleash its power unless we absolutely have to."

"Do you have any idea if we can control it?" I ask. "You're the Kah-Gash's memory. Is there anything you can tell us about how it functioned in the past?"

Bec shakes her head. "I've always had a perfect memory, and now I can absorb the memories of others. This explains why. But I can only recall the memories of my own life or the lives of those I touch. Perhaps, if we joined, the Kah-Gash would reveal more to me, but the dangers..."

"What dangers?" Grubbs snorts. "We're wrong to be afraid. This is *our* weapon. We own the pieces — hell, we *are* the pieces. We're the Kah-Gash's masters."

"No," I correct him. "We're its *hosts*. The pieces have been in thousands of other creatures before. We have no more claim over it than any of them did."

"Let's just do it," Grubbs groans. "It wants to be

used. I feel my piece straining to link with yours."

"I feel that too," Bec says, "and it scares me. Why is it so eager to be restored, now, after all this time, with Death on the loose and hordes of demons bearing down on our world? It could be plotting against us."

"It did what we wanted when we linked before," Grubbs protests. "It took us back in time so that we could stop the tunnel being opened."

"What if that was a mistake?" Bec argues. "What if we join again and it takes us further back, to when this universe was born? What if it stops that?"

Grubbs scowls and looks away impatiently.

"I share Bec's concerns," I tell them. "Even the Old Creatures don't know what the Kah-Gash is really like, and they've been studying it for billions of years. We can't know its true intentions."

"Can we afford to wait?" Dervish asks. "If we're as close to the end as the Old Creatures predict... I think we should test it."

I sigh. "If it goes wrong, we'll be condemning all those creatures on the ark."

"This will sound callous," Meera says, "but I don't care. If our world ends, for me *everything* ends. I'm not concerned about other planets, Old Creatures or aliens. You feel that way too, Kernel. You wouldn't have come back if you didn't."

"But there are so many worlds... so many species..."

"Tough," Meera snorts. "They're not our problem. You came back to help save Earth, not the universe. Am I right or am I right?"

I smile weakly. "I can't argue with that. OK, I'll give it a go. But if I start to think we can't beat Death – if it looks like we're fighting a losing battle – I *will* return to the ark. I won't go down with a sinking ship."

Dervish claps my back. "I think you were mad to return, but I like your style! Here's what I suggest. We move on to the city where the next crossing's going to happen and we let the window open. You three link and test yourselves against the demons. If you don't wreck the universe, we'll take that experience forward and confront the Shadow. If you *do* wreck the universe… well, we'll all be dead, so we won't have to worry about it. How does that sound?"

"Good to me," Grubbs grunts.

I shrug.

"I suppose," Bec says hesitantly. "But assuming we pass the test, I'd like to try and learn more about Death before we attack it, find out if it has any weaknesses, if there's a way to defeat it."

"How are we supposed to do that?" Grubbs sneers. "Send it a questionnaire?"

Bec licks her lips nervously. "We might have an inside man who can help us."

"What are you talking about?" Dervish frowns.

"It's something Beranabus said before he died." Bec shudders. She was close to the old magician. His death hit her hard. "In the hold of the ship, after I told him about Death, he said to tell Kernel to find him."

"He wanted me to open a window out of the hold," I mutter, feeling guilty even though I know there's nothing I could have done to help him.

"That's what I thought," Bec nods. "I assumed he planned to escape or knock the lodestone through the window. But the more I think about it, the more I doubt that assumption. He knew he couldn't last long against the Shadow, that it would take us several minutes to climb the stairs. He knew you were part of the Kah-Gash and that the Shadow wanted to get its hands on you. Why would he ask you to risk capture? He was doomed and he accepted his death. His only concern was that we evade the Shadow and live to fight another day.

"I don't think he was asking for help." Bec licks her lips again. "I think he was looking ahead. Once he knew what the Shadow was, he resigned himself to dying. But he didn't give up the fight. Juni and I are proof that death isn't the end. When he found out who his enemy was, I believe Beranabus saw a chance to learn more about it and share that information with us.

"Death uses souls to create its body. Maybe it held on to Beranabus's soul when it killed him. Part of him might be alive inside that monstrous mass of shadows."

Bec looks at me and grins shakily. "You can locate anything in the universes of the living, Kernel. Do you think you could find a ghost in the realm of the dead?"

# SHADES OF THE FALLEN

→There's uproar when Bec suggests Beranabus might still be alive in some form. Grubbs accuses her of living in dreamland. Meera gently suggests that she's in denial, that she needs to accept the ancient magician's death. But Bec stubbornly pushes her case, and as she elaborates, our scepticism fades.

We know souls can be separated from bodies — that happened to me in Lord Loss's kingdom years ago, when I entered the Board. In the past, a soul couldn't survive a body's death, but things have changed. Death is claiming souls and using them. We've no way of knowing if a captured soul remains conscious or not. But if they do... if Beranabus has made a study of Death from the inside and uncovered its secrets... maybe he can tell us how to kill it.

It's probably a wild shot in the dark. Grubbs certainly thinks so and says that it's a waste of time, but the rest of us believe it's worth trying.

But before we can set off in pursuit of a dead man,

we have the living to take care of. The new window is almost open. In another few hours, dozens of demons will be streaming across.

While Grubbs fetches his werewolves and Meera rustles up battle-hardened soldiers, I slot patches of light together. Dervish and Kirilli are resting — Dervish looks shattered, Kirilli scared. Bec's watching me. Something about her gaze makes me feel uneasy.

"It must have been amazing," she says. "Your trip to the stars and beyond sounds incredible."

"Yes," I grunt.

"I was wondering…" She coughs. "I'd like to touch you."

"What?" I squeak, startled, thinking she wants to kiss me.

"I can absorb your memories if we touch," she says.

"Oh." I chuckle at my mistake. Then I grow serious. "Why do you want to take my memories?"

"Not take," she says. "Share. I want to see everything you saw. The lights, the worlds, the Crux. If you grant me access, I can see all that you did."

"What does it matter if I show you or not?" I snap.

She looks surprised by my harsh tone. "Well, of course I'm curious," she says, stammering a bit. "But apart from that I have perfect recall. If you share with me, I might spot something that slipped your mind."

"I doubt it," I sniff.

"But it can't do any harm, surely, if I just..." She reaches out, then stops as I glare at her. Letting her hand drop slowly, her expression darkens. "You're hiding something from us. Just like Grubbs."

"You saw that too?" I hiss.

"Everyone sees it. Something happened between him and Juni that he doesn't want us to know."

"What do you think it might be?" I ask.

"I've no idea. But I think I know what *you're* holding back. You look hostile. I've done nothing to make you dislike me, so you must be... afraid."

"I'm not afraid of you," I sneer.

"Maybe not. But you're nervous... more than that... *suspicious?*"

I fidget uncomfortably.

"The Old Creatures said the pieces of the Kah-Gash have been influenced by the hosts they've inhabited," Bec says thoughtfully. "If my piece of the Kah-Gash was in Lord Loss for thousands of years..." Her expression clears. "You don't trust me. You think I might betray you, or that my piece of the Kah-Gash might trick us."

"Can you say for sure that it won't?" I ask quietly.

Bec starts to respond hotly, then pauses. "Actually no," she admits. Then she looks at me piercingly. "But can *you* make any guarantees? Can Grubbs? You don't know where your pieces were before, or why they ended up in you. Maybe we'll all be played for fools."

"Maybe." I nod slowly.

Bec smiles thinly. "Go on watching me, Kernel. I don't mind. But I'll be watching you too. And Grubbs. I don't think any of us can be trusted."

"You're right," I say glumly, then return her smile. "And *we're* the ones who are supposed to save the world? I don't fancy our chances!"

"Me neither," she laughs, and we grin at each other, united by our uncertainties, paranoia and fear.

→We could stop the mage before he opens the window, but then we wouldn't have a chance to test ourselves. I don't like the course we're taking – people will probably die – but there's no other way. If we want to learn about the Kah-Gash before we go looking for the Shadow, we have to fight. We could cross to the demon universe and test it there, but that would mean unleashing the Kah-Gash in an area of total magic. If the weapon's on the side of the Demonata, that would hand it the perfect opportunity to break free of any confines we might seek to impose.

"Stick close to me," Grubbs growls. I'm on his left, Bec on his right. Meera, Kirilli, the werewolves and soldiers are behind us. Dervish is a bit further back, observing. I sense the window forming. Just minutes to go. The mage is working inside a nearby building.

"We're not going for a full union," Grubbs says. "Just a partial link."

"Are you sure we can do that?" I ask.

"Yes," Grubbs says. "I'm the trigger. I can control it. Follow my lead, don't react when you feel my magic mingling with yours, and everything will be coolio."

I share a troubled glance with Bec – she doesn't like this either – but before I can say anything the window opens and demons scurry out of the building. There are dozens of scaly, bloody, multi-headed monsters, oozing pus and slime, slithering down the steps, smashing through windows, hunting for victims. A river of nightmares.

But nothing new. I faced worse with Beranabus. I'm more concerned about the werewolf between me and Bec than I am by the demons bearing down on us.

Grubbs stares at the Demonata, eyes narrow and glinting yellow. His fangs grow an inch, his lips stretching with them. He grabs hold of my hand and Bec's. Energy spirals up my arm. I tense against it but then the voice of the Kah-Gash murmurs to me. *It's all right. Don't fight. No harm will come of this.*

I don't entirely trust that inner voice, but even if I wanted to reject the union, I couldn't. The magic within me warms to Grubbs's and I feel power well up from nowhere. The shock of it makes me gasp. My skin crackles and my fingers dig into Grubbs's huge paw. My legs go weak, then steady.

We're drawing power from all around, from the earth, people, demons, the sky. Everything's linked. There are connecting lines everywhere, between humans, objects, the Demonata, the stars. The Kah-Gash was here before any of us, holding the sixty-four zones of the original universe together. And it still binds us in place — it just doesn't define the universes as tightly as it used to.

But it could. With the power coursing through me now, I could quench the sun by snapping my fingers, and open a tunnel between universes. Make myself ruler of all worlds, people and demons. Limits exist only in the mind. As the Kah-Gash, I'd set those limits, not be bound by them. I could–

"Let's just kill these demons and leave it at that," Grubbs says, shattering my dreams of universal dominance.

I blink, coming out of the spell I was under, amazed by how swiftly I gave in to temptation. Grubbs and Bec might not be the jokers in the pack. Maybe *I'm* the weak link, the one the Kah-Gash can exploit.

But there's no time for self-doubt. The demons are almost upon us. Our werewolves are howling and the soldiers are readying their rifles. Another second or two and all will be chaos.

Grubbs roars and I feel the magic of the Kah-Gash

draining from me — from Bec too. Grubbs is the focal point through which the power is channelled. No way of fighting it now. The energy that we've sucked in explodes through Grubbs, mixed in with his roar.

A stream of raw power envelops the demons and stops them cold. Their eyes bulge as they choke in a net of magic. We hold them in place a moment, as easily as we'd trap a colony of ants by lowering a jar over them. Then Grubbs blows on them the way he'd blow on a feather.

The demons shoot backwards, through the walls of the building, then through the window between universes. The startled mage is blasted through as well, torn to shreds with most of the demons. When the area is clear, the stream of energy fans out and crackles across the face of the window. It glows brightly, then crumples, and the patches of light which were used to create it flood back to us along with the magic. The stream swirls around us, breaking up into vortex-like tendrils. Then Grubbs lets go of my hand and Bec's.

The power dwindles in seconds and the lights drift away. It's like nothing ever happened — apart from the huge hole in the front of the building.

"Wow," Grubbs says, flexing his fingers and staring at them. "That was great." He looks up at us and grins. "Let's find more demons and do it again!"

→A couple of hours later, in a hotel suite even grander than the last we stayed in, Grubbs is still itching to pick another fight, but Bec insists we should focus on Beranabus. The pair are arguing heatedly. I've kept quiet. Dervish, Meera and Kirilli say nothing either. We chipped in during the early stages of the argument, but for the last hour it's been pretty much Grubbs and Bec yelling at each other.

"Forget about crossing!" Grubbs shouts, towering over the small, slender girl. "I say we wait for them to come. With the power of the Kah-Gash, we'll drive them back every time. They'll soon realise they can't win and head off for softer pickings on other worlds."

"You think that's acceptable?" Bec retorts, not intimidated by the grotesque, wolfen teenager. "We pass them along and let others suffer?"

"Like Meera said, we only care about this world," Grubbs huffs.

"Leave me out of this," Meera snaps, but both ignore her.

"What about Death?" Bec jeers. "Will you repel the Shadow when it attacks?"

"Why not? Death might be more powerful than the Demonata, but the Kah-Gash can trump it."

"No," Bec says. "Death is the ultimate power. If we don't strike now, it will grow stronger and come to find us."

Grubbs shrugs. "Do I look worried?"

Bec smothers a curse. "You were all for attacking earlier. You wanted to go for Death like a dog after a rat."

"That was before you brought Beranabus into the equation. I'd still go if you only wanted to have a crack at the Shadow. But you want to free a dead man. That's what this is really about. Your beloved *Bran* turned coward at the end."

"What are you talking about?" Bec screeches and appeals to the rest of us. "Has he gone mad? Do any of you know what–"

"Beranabus was afraid," Grubbs interrupts. "That's why he told you to send Kernel after him. It wasn't so he could study Death from the inside and learn its secrets. He realised his soul might be trapped and he didn't want to spend eternity in the grasp of the Shadow. He hoped Kernel could get him out. You know that's true. You knew it from the moment you suggested the idea of rescuing him. Tell me I'm wrong."

Bec says nothing. Her face was red with anger moments before, but now the flush fades. Her lower jaw trembles. She looks ashamed.

"This is personal," Grubbs growls, facing us like a lawyer addressing a jury. "She's not thinking about beating Death. She only wants to set Beranabus free."

"What's wrong with that?" Meera asks quietly. "He was her friend. You'd do the same for Dervish in that position. So would I."

"I wouldn't," Kirilli pipes up.

"No surprise there," Dervish mutters.

"It's too dangerous," Grubbs yells. "I liked Beranabus but I'm not going to risk everything to save his soul. Hell, he might not even be there. Maybe Death didn't claim him."

"It did," I say softly. "I've been studying the lights while you were arguing, concentrating on Beranabus. A few started flashing as soon as I focused on him, and more have joined them. It's not like when I search for someone living, but if his soul hadn't been absorbed by the Shadow, no lights would flash at all."

"OK, it took his soul. So what?" Grubbs shrugs. "How many of you want to risk a rescue? Who cared about the mad old buzzard that much?"

He looks around the room. Kirilli instantly shakes his head. Meera nods firmly to show she's on Bec's side. Dervish looks uncertain. "We owe him," he says.

"We owe a lot of people," Grubbs grunts, "but we can't always repay our debts. You taught me that. A Disciple doesn't risk his life to save a few people, not when the fate of billions is at stake.

"If I think we have a real chance of hurting the Shadow, I'll jump at it. But if we're just going over there to free Beranabus's soul... That's not right. Beranabus wouldn't have thought so either — not until he crumbled at the end."

"What if he didn't?" I ask angrily. "I spent more time with him than any of you. I never saw him ask for favours. He was the most selfless person I knew. What if he really did hope to learn something that might help us?"

"I'm not willing to take that chance," Grubbs says.

"You're a fool!" Bec shouts.

"Maybe," Grubbs sniffs. "But it looks like we have a tie, three votes for each. You, Meera and Kernel want to ride to the rescue. Kirilli and I have more sense. And Dervish..." He looks to his uncle for a final answer.

Dervish sighs. "I agree with Grubbs. We can't let personal feelings cloud our judgement."

"What if it was personal for *you?*" I softly challenge him.

"It's not," Dervish says wearily. "If Grubbs was in that position, I'd do all I could to free him. But he isn't, so there's no point–"

"*Bill-E*," Bec stops him. Dervish turns slowly, left eyelid ticking, but she isn't looking at him. She's staring at me. "Is it Bill-E?"

I nod slowly.

"Liar!" Grubbs howls, raising a huge, shaggy fist. "How dare you–"

"I searched for him after I looked for Beranabus," I say quickly. "I was running tests, searching for others I knew who'd died, like Mrs Egin, Logan Rile, Sharmila. I came up blank on all of them. Then I thought of Bill-E and a few lights flashed, the way they flashed for Beranabus."

"If you're lying…" Grubbs growls, fingers clenched tight.

I step forward. I'm shaking like a rattlesnake's tail but I speak clearly. "If you think I'd say this to trick you, you don't know me at all."

Grubbs stares into my eyes. He wants to find deception, but he can't because I'm telling the truth. His shoulders slump and he backs away. He shares a scared look with Dervish, who's been hit just as hard by the news.

Bec could crow, but she doesn't. She merely waits.

"I killed him to free him," Grubbs finally croaks. "It was the hardest thing I've done. I murdered my own brother. I wouldn't have done that to save the world, the universe or anything else. But I couldn't bear to let him live in torment at the hands of the Demonata. I killed him to spare his suffering, to set him free. Now you're telling me I didn't, that the Shadow has him?"

"I'm sorry," I whisper.

Tears of blood trickle from Grubbs's eyes. Raising

a hand, he wipes them away, then covers his face with his hand and moans softly.

"We have to free them," Bec says. She crouches by his side and reaches out to embrace him.

"Don't touch me!" he barks, pulling away from her.

"Don't be silly," she smiles. "I absorbed your secret when we linked outside. I know what Juni predicted. But I don't believe her. She's insane. You would never do what she claimed."

Grubbs cries out and wraps his arms around the little girl, hugging her like a doll, weeping while we stare at the pair of them, bewildered. When he finally stops crying, he releases Bec and grins shakily at her, then casts his gaze over the rest of us, his features firm.

"Show of hands. Who's going to help me and Bec kick some Shadow ass?"

Five arms rise immediately. Kirilli is the only dissenter. "You're all mad," he grumbles.

"Overruled," Dervish laughs, then twists his spikes into place and drawls like a gangster. "I always wanted to be part of a jailbreak!"

# THE CARRIAGE HELD...

→I try opening a window to Beranabus, then Bill-E, but enjoy no luck. It's too difficult on this world. The lights are few and scattered. I need more power to piece them together. I need the magic of the demon universe.

We cross to a realm we know is safe, where we've based ourselves in the past. Grubbs brings his pack of werewolves along ("For fun," he grins bleakly) but we leave the soldiers behind. I choose a place where time operates like it does on Earth. That way we should be back to face the next assault. Assuming we survive our brush with Death. Which is a pretty big assumption.

As the others prepare for battle, I use the lights to pinpoint the position of our enemies. I still can't get a fix on Death, even though I now know its identity. But I find Lord Loss and Juni Swan easily enough. They're on a world I've never been to, surrounded by thousands... no, *millions* of demons. The thought of entering the midst of such an army is terrifying.

I think of telling the others, but what's the point? We have to do this. Bec, Dervish and Grubbs for personal reasons, me because I believe – *hope* – Beranabus can reveal something about Death which will give us the power to defeat it. If all goes well, we won't have to face the demons, just their shadowy master. If it goes poorly...

Best not to dwell on that.

I turn my thoughts away from demons. Breathing calmly, I focus on Beranabus. Lights begin to pulse, but there aren't many of them and I have a tough time piecing them together. Normally lights flock to me when I summon them, but these patches resist. I have to focus harder than I've ever had to, and even then they only drift towards me sluggishly, reluctantly.

Gritting my teeth, I bully the patches into place, slotting them together as if they were pieces of a crudely carved jigsaw puzzle. I'm aware of time ticking, the others growing impatient, especially the werewolves, who howl and hammer the ground with their fists, eager for action.

I push the distractions from my mind and focus on the lights. Normally I can multi-task, chat with others while I'm working on a window. Not now. This will take everything I have. I'm doing something no one has ever done before, breaching the barriers of life itself.

Eventually, after hours of fierce concentration,

when I'm starting to think it's impossible, a small window opens. It's an unimpressive, jagged panel of brown light, and it flickers alarmingly at the edges. But I don't care. It shouldn't by rights be open at all, so I'm more proud of it than any window I've ever created.

"Come on!" I shout, reacting quickly to push the outermost lights back in place before they can buckle. "This will only hold for a few seconds."

"Where does it–" Grubbs starts to ask.

"No time!" I yell. "We have to go *now* or not at all."

"Then let's go," Grubbs grunts and dives blindly through the window.

The werewolves rush after him. When the last of the sixteen has vanished, a nervous Meera crosses, followed by Bec. Kirilli steps forward, but hesitates.

"I really don't want to do this," he mutters.

"Too bad!" Dervish laughs and pushes the startled stage magician through.

"Hurry," I gasp, feeling the window start to disintegrate.

Dervish ducks past my whirring arms. As soon as he's out of sight, I throw myself after him. I sense the window collapse as I sail through. Whatever happens next, whatever dire mess we wind up in, there's no quick way out. We're in this to the end whether we like it or not

→I find myself in a realm of shadows, dark and swirling. The shadows whip at me and then flit away as if blown by a strong wind. But there's no wind here, just the ever-circling shades of the dead.

I was expecting cries and moans of torment, but it's silent. That surprises me. At the least I should be able to hear the howls of the werewolves. But when I open my mouth to call for the others – I can't see any of them – I realise why it's so quiet. Sounds don't carry. Though I shout at the top of my voice, nothing emerges.

I hunker down, fighting the dark wisps which threaten to bowl me over and sweep me away. There's no floor, just banks of shadows all around. I'm not floating. It's more like being stuck in a pool of mud.

I try to create a ball of light, but nothing happens. There's magic here, waves of energy washing between the shadowy souls and binding them, but it's a different type of magic and I'm unable to channel it.

As I try again, something solid strikes my left shoulder. Cringing away from my assailant, I peer through the streams of shadows masking my eyes. I spy a bulky shape bearing down on me. Impossible to tell if it's friend or foe. I back up, desperately scouring the space around me for a trace of magic I can use. Then a pair of huge hands grasps my arms and tugs me to a halt. A face thrusts up next to mine. It's a fearsome, demonic face and my first instinct is to lash out. But as a veil of shadows whisks away from over the creature's eyes, I realise it's Grubbs.

He says something. I shake my head and mouth back the words, "I can't hear."

Grubbs narrows his eyes. Nothing happens for a few seconds. Then I hear his voice inside my head. "–me now? Can you hear me now? Can you–"

"Yes," I stop him, replying silently, thinking the words instead of voicing them.

"Are you able to channel the magic?" he asks.

"No."

He tuts, then grins. "I couldn't either. Nobody could. But Bec adapted swiftly and showed the rest of us. Come on."

He leads me through the shadows, half-staggering, half-swimming. The others aren't far away, grouped together, Bec at the centre, the rest huddled round her, lit dimly by flickering balls of light which she has generated. They all look scared, especially Kirilli. Even the werewolves are subdued, whining silently and glancing around uneasily.

Once I'm in physical contact with the group, Bec speaks. "We haven't much time. Death isn't aware of us yet but it will discover us soon. You have to find Beranabus and Bill-E as quickly as possible."

I realise she's talking to me. "How can I find them?"

I protest. "I opened the window and brought us here. What more can I do?"

"You're the eyes of the Kah-Gash," she snaps. "You see more than any of us. To me there's no difference in the shadows. They all look the same. But I'm sure you can see more."

"Well, I can't," I snarl, hating the way she's heaping the pressure on to me.

A wave of energy floods through me, opening doors within my brain, clearing passageways. Suddenly I find myself absorbing and converting the magic of Death. I fill with power and breathe out easily, smiling at the buzz of it.

"How did you do that?" I ask, relaxed and cool.

"I used my gift," Bec says. "Now use yours and *look*."

Still smiling, I cast my gaze around and see that Bec was right. Now that I've tapped into the magic, the shadows have taken on a new consistency. There are thousands of individual shards and shapes whirling around us, no two alike. I can't believe I didn't see them before. Each has its own shade, form and way of moving. They're all a grey-black colour, but there are more variants of grey and black than I would have dreamt possible.

My first thought is, "So this is what souls look like." But that's not right. This is only what they look like *here*. Death has taken these unfortunates and moulded them into what it wanted them to be.

As I study the souls, I extend my thoughts, focusing on individuals, trying to communicate. Nothing happens for a while. Then, all of a sudden, I'm struck by a burst of voices, screams and yowls, tormented cries for help and release. Wincing, I shut out the noises. After a brief pause, I open myself to the voices again, but put filters in place, blocking out the worst of the background noise.

"Who are you?" I ask a nearby shadow as it floats past.

"Free me!" it screams.

"Who are you?" I shout again, but it only repeats its plea. Others that I focus on are the same, impossible to question, wailing for freedom.

I turn to tell the others, but I don't need to. Bec has been in touch with me the whole time and has broadcast the short snippets to the rest. They look distraught. The suffering of these souls is awful. In life, no matter how bad things get, at least you have the release of death to look forward to, the belief that no matter what lies beyond, nothing can be as bad as *this*.

But these people have shuffled off their mortal coils, only to find themselves ensnared by the force they were relying on to set them free. Every soul here knows it wasn't meant for this hellish realm. Having escaped the confines of natural life, they've found themselves caught in an unnatural web and it's driven them mad.

"We have to get out of here!" Kirilli shrieks. "We can't help them!"

"Bran won't have given in to madness," Bec insists. "Find him, Kernel. He won't have surrendered. Not Bran."

I don't have her faith in the ancient magician, but I search anyway. Using the magic of Death, I send a radar-like cry out in all directions, calling for Beranabus, trying to locate his position. Once I've sent the signal, I wait for it to echo back. If he's still conscious, he'll respond. But if he's like the others... if he's lost his senses and forgotten his name... become just a swirling shadow with no idea of self...

"Bill-E," Grubbs snarls as we wait. "Look for Bill-E too."

"I will," I tell him, "but give me time. Beranabus first. If we–"

I stop, jaw dropping. Because an answering burst of energy has echoed back to me from a point far away.

"Was that Bran?" Bec hisses.

"I think so," I say hesitantly. "But it was very weak. I guess there's only one way to find out." I look around to make sure everyone's ready, then start forward, wading through the sluggish swirls of shadows, repeating the signal, zoning in on the area where the soul of Beranabus seems to be signalling back.

→We reach the place where the response came from. I don't see anything different at first. It looks like any other part of this wretched no-man's-land. The souls cluster and swirl around us. I call Beranabus's name, but there's no reply. I study the river of souls, but it's impossible to say who they might have belonged to in life. Maybe the reply was a fluke, or I only heard –

"That was always your problem," a voice snaps inside my head. "You take too many things into consideration."

"Bran!" Bec cries, head whipping from side to side, searching the gloom for her childhood friend.

"I'm here," Beranabus says, and I trace the voice to a shadow circling overhead, no more remarkable than any other.

"Where is he?" Bec shouts. "I can't see him."

"Relax, Little One," Beranabus hushes her. "Kernel's the only one who can see me. You'll have to be content with my voice. Not that it's a bad voice. I've roared down demon masters in my time."

I burst out laughing. This is the most incredible thing ever. I never thought I'd be in direct contact with my old mentor again. But before I can tell him how sorry I am that he was killed, Grubbs shouts at the dead magician.

"Is Bill-E here?" he cries.

"Aye," Beranabus rumbles.

"Where? Let me talk with him. Bill-E!" Grubbs swivels wildly, shouting his dead brother's name.

"Were you always this stupid or is it a result of your recent metamorphosis?" Beranabus snaps. "I was thousands of years old when I died, more powerful than any human in history. Yet it took everything I had to hold my thoughts together and not become one of the wailing cretins this place is stuffed with. Do you really think your young brother fought off the madness that all the others succumbed to?"

Grubbs draws to a stop and turns to face me, his eyes cold with hatred. "Show me where that vile old buzzard is. I'll kill him again."

Beranabus laughs cruelly. "Control yourself. I never put things politely when I was alive, so I'm hardly going to start now that I'm dead! Your brother's here, he's lost his mind and is suffering, and unless you free us all, he'll remain trapped indefinitely."

"Then we *can* free you?" Bec shouts hopefully.

"I think so," Beranabus mutters. "That's not why I told you to ask Kernel to find me, but it will certainly be a bonus. I can't hold my mind together much longer. The effort..." In those few words I get the sense of how close Beranabus is to snapping. Despite his brave front, he's terrified.

"Before we try that," Beranabus says more brightly,

"I want to know everything that's happened since I died. Bec — open your thoughts to me."

The shadow of Beranabus's soul darts closer to Bec and hovers over the girl's head. A tendril gently touches her forehead. She closes her eyes and smiles. I get the impression of memories being transferred, like data being uploaded from one computer to another. Then Beranabus sighs.

"I'd gathered some of that already – you can learn a lot here if you keep your eyes and ears open, metaphorically speaking – but there's much more to consider now. I don't think..."

He falls silent. Bec's eyes half open, then close again. She nods softly and I realise he's speaking privately to her.

Grubbs steps up beside me. "Can you find Bill-E?" he asks.

"Even if I could, would you want to speak to him like this?" I answer quietly. "Wouldn't it be better to just free him?"

"But I never said a proper goodbye. There are so many things–"

"Kernel's right," Dervish says, laying a trembling hand on Grubbs's shoulder. "Better to remember Bill-E as he was. If we can set his soul loose, that will be enough."

Grubbs nods reluctantly, then squints at Bec.

"What's going on between those two? Why the secrecy?"

"I was wondering the same thing," I whisper.

"Such suspicious minds," Beranabus barks. "You'll need to trust each other if you're to defeat Death and save the universe. Haven't you heard of teamwork?"

"You think we *can* beat it?" I ask eagerly.

"Not a hope in hell," Beranabus chuckles. "But you have to try, don't you?"

Bec's eyes are open. She looks troubled. I don't know what Beranabus shared with her, but I'm reminded of Raz's warning. I have a bad feeling. Suddenly I wish I hadn't insisted on this mission, that I'd left Beranabus alone. I thought he could teach us how to vanquish our foes, but all he's done is predict doom and tell Bec something that's set her mind awhirl. But awhirl with what? *Deceit?*

Before I can press the issue, a cluster of shadows to my left bunch together, throb, then rise high above us like a cobra's head.

"Ah," Beranabus sighs. "The behemoth awakes."

"It's alive!" Kirilli shrieks as the shadowy growth studies us ominously.

"This would be a good time to split," Meera mutters.

The pillar of shadows smashes down on us before anyone can volunteer a plan. We're thrown apart, yelling with panic. The werewolves howl and lurch at the massed head of shadows, but it bats them aside with ease and rises above us again. As it does, more shadows converge around us. Death might have taken a while to note our presence, but it's moving swiftly to turn its imprisoned souls against us.

"Bec!" I roar, dodging another of the Shadow's blows. "How do we get out?"

Beranabus answers mockingly. "Can't you open a window, Kernel? That was always your speciality."

"No time!" I yell. "Bec?"

"The Kah-Gash," she says shakily, reaching towards me. A twisting fist of shadows slams into her right arm, snapping it at the elbow. She screams as her hand goes limp, then grits her teeth and unleashes a burst of energy at the fist. The shadows shatter beneath the force of the blow. Bec clutches me with her left hand. "Grubbs!" she yells.

He's already making his way towards us, lips moving silently as he speaks to his piece of the Kah-Gash. A sword of shadows slices across his back, drawing blood, but he just grunts and pushes on.

Kirilli's bouncing about like a Mexican jumping bean, dodging the spines and hammers that are forming and striking at us, yelping with each narrow escape, the rags of his tattered suit flapping up and down to comical effect.

"That's the way," Beranabus laughs at the petrified stage magician. "Dance, fool, dance!" He cackles madly. I think he's closer to insanity than he realises.

Grubbs reaches us and lays a powerful paw on my neck, the other on Bec's. I immediately feel the Kah-Gash flare into life. There's not as much power as before because we're surrounded by Death, unable to draw energy from the stars. But I still feel about ten times more powerful than normal.

As a hammer of shadows crashes upon us, Grubbs roars and it disintegrates. He releases Bec and me but the link remains. With his hands, he claws at the shadows around us, ripping dark holes through the fog of souls. Bec and I follow his lead, using magic to split shadows and blast through thicker banks of them. The others join in – except Kirilli, who's still leaping about – and we attack the formations that Death has sent against us.

"This way," Beranabus calls, shooting ahead. I don't know how anyone could find their bearings here, but I have to trust him. It's not like we have much choice.

We struggle after the fleeing shadow. I'm following Beranabus, the others are trailing me. Kirilli is the only one who doesn't come. He hasn't looked around. I call his name a few times, but he doesn't respond. In the end I curse and leave him. I feel bad, abandoning the Disciple, but you can't save everyone. Some of the werewolves have already been killed. The power of the Kah-Gash is fading, having no outside source to draw from. If I went back for Kirilli, I'd waste energy and time, and that would prove the death of us all.

A noise grows as we push on. It's a hissing sound, the spitting of a million furious snakes. Death is venting its rage. I've heard all sorts of shrieks and cries during my years in the demon universe. Nothing sent a shiver down my spine as much as this.

A spear of shadows strikes Grubbs just above his heart and shoots out the other side. With a roar of pain he falls to his knees, but is up again instantly. His fangs lengthen and as another spear arcs towards him, he snatches it between his oversized teeth and grinds it to pieces, then spits them out.

A shadowy scythe splits the flesh of Meera's lower back. She staggers, finds her feet, then is struck by a thick club. She falls unconscious, but Dervish is there to grab her and haul her forwards. His face is flushed, his limbs are trembling, his heart must be pounding fit to burst, but he carries on. I don't know if it's for Meera's sake or his own, but he doesn't quit, even though it would be easier for him to lie down and die.

I've been hammered all over and I'm bleeding from a variety of cuts, like the others, but Bec's hardly been touched. She's the strongest of us in this place of death. Grubbs might be the trigger, but Bec is pulling the strings at the moment, directing the energy of the Kah-Gash, using it to keep the lights going, protect herself from the blows of the Shadow, and help the rest of us as best she can. For such a small girl, she packs one hell of a lot of power.

"Here!" Beranabus calls. He's come to a halt by a thick bank of souls. "This is a wall. Focus on this spot. Quickly — you're almost out of time."

Bec unleashes a ball of energy at the wall. I do the same. Grubbs starts to, then snarls and hurls himself at it instead. He hits the bank of shadows and rips into it, roaring as he scoops dark handfuls out of his way. The surviving werewolves crowd around him and tear at the shadows too.

"Nearly there!" Beranabus roars cheerfully as Dervish and Meera are knocked aside, and I narrowly avoid being speared through the centre of my head.

A hole appears in the side of the Shadow. Light shines through, blinding after the gloominess of this unnatural realm. The werewolves howl gleefully and double their efforts. The hole widens and I hit it with another blast of energy. Bec focuses on the area around it. Grubbs rips at the shadows like a madman. More holes and tears appear. Some of the souls drift free and disappear as they hit the air outside. Others follow, streaming after the first few. The holes widen, then the fabric around them crumbles away. The hissing reaches its peak, only now it's a scream of pain. Souls dart from their prison, sensing escape, surging towards the exit from all parts of Death's makeshift body.

Beranabus yodels enthusiastically, fighting the flow, holding his position. "Not bad," he chuckles approvingly.

"Is that it?" I cry, hardly daring to believe it could be this simple. "Have we killed Death?"

"Don't be ridiculous," Beranabus snorts. "Death can't die."

"But conscious Death… the Shadow… have we destroyed it?" I yell.

"No," Beranabus says sadly, sounding more like his old self. "You've delayed matters, that's all. It will have to find new souls and create another body. That will take weeks, maybe a month or two. Then it will be back, stronger than ever. Having learnt from this setback, it will be more vigilant. You won't pierce its defences so easily again."

"Then how will we beat it?" I shriek. "How will we win?"

"You won't," Beranabus whispers. Then he's gone, whipped free of his prison, cheering wildly, to depart the universe of the living once and for all, bound for whatever lies beyond. Bec yells a frantic farewell, but

I don't think he hears. He doesn't care about life now or those who inhabit it. He's done.

As I stare at the souls flying past, shocked by Beranabus's parting prophecy, Death's brittle shell dissolves and I fall through the layers of shadow on to hard, dry land — and drop into the middle of an army of millions of demons.

# SWAN SONG

→Ranks of monsters surround us, stretching far into the distance. This must be the world from which the Demonata are plotting their invasion of Earth, the base from which they send troops when they open windows to our world. We knew an army was massing, but we never dared confront it. Beranabus was a reckless fighter, but he wasn't crazy. He knew we couldn't hope to face this many demons and walk away alive.

The demons have backed off from the disintegrating mammoth of the Shadow. They're watching it with alarm, chittering and bellowing, not sure what's going on. It's their leader. Death drew them together, promising them control of the universe and eternal life. Now it's falling to pieces like a punctured Zeppelin. They don't know what to do.

"*There!*" shrieks an all too recognisable voice. Pushing myself to my feet, I spy her near the fore of the demons to my left — Nadia Moore, aka Juni

Swan. She's by the side of her eight-armed master, Lord Loss. Both are staring at us with a mix of hatred and uncertainty.

I look around slowly, showing no signs of panic in case I incite the Demonata. Grubbs and Bec are nearby. Grubbs has also seen Juni and Lord Loss. He's taking deep breaths, preparing for battle. Bec is fixing her arm and doesn't seem to be aware of the trouble we're in. Dervish is using magic to revive Meera, glancing around anxiously as he fans her back to life. The ten surviving werewolves have gathered in a circle behind Grubbs, growling softly as they eyeball the demons. And a little further over, hopping around, unaware that we've escaped the stomach of the Shadow, is Kirilli Kovacs.

"Grubbs," I hiss. "Any ideas?"

"Can you open a window?" he mutters, cracking his knuckles.

"I've already started," I whisper, nudging patches of light into place with deft flicks of my fingers, not wanting to alert our enemies to the fact that I'm at work. "It'll take a few minutes. Can you cover me?"

"I'll give it a good shot," he growls, then bellows at Lord Loss. "Where's your mighty leader now? Death offered you the universe and immortality. Hah!"

Bec finishes setting her arm and calmly walks over to Grubbs. She stands behind him, back to back.

Dervish and a woozy Meera shuffle up beside them. When Kirilli hears Grubbs, he stops dancing and stares around. The werewolves haven't moved, awaiting Grubbs's command.

"Very commendable, Grubitsch," Lord Loss says. His voice silences the mutterings and snarls of the other demons. He drifts to the front of the army, Juni by his side. When he's in the open, he looks at each of us in turn and smiles. "But Death cannot be destroyed. You have merely inconvenienced it. A valiant victory, but you have only won a battle, not the war. You know that. We *all* know that." He addresses the last cry to the army of demons, raising his voice, and they roar back encouragingly.

"This feels like a reunion," Lord Loss says, smiling sadly, the snakes writhing in the hole where his heart should be, blood oozing from the many cracks in his pale red flesh. "So many familiar faces. Grubitsch, Dervish, Cornelius, even little Bec, back from the dead and as tenacious as ever."

"Master," Juni murmurs, nodding sharply at me.

"I am aware of Cornelius's efforts," Lord Loss chuckles. "Don't worry, sweet Swan, he will not have time to open a window. I let him get this far in order to fan the flames of hope in their hearts. Now that those flames are flickering nicely–" His red eyes flash dangerously. "–it is time to quench them." He shouts at the millions of demons, "*Attack!*"

With a volley of deafening screams and howls, the army surges forward and smashes to the ground around us, a living wave of chaos, barbarism and death.

→We'd perish in seconds without the power of the Kah-Gash. But as soon as Lord Loss roars, Grubbs grabs Bec, leaps to my side and wraps an arm around me. Unifying our magic, he draws from the power in the air and erects a hasty but sturdy barrier around us. Instead of driving us to the floor and ripping us to shreds, the demons deflect off the shield.

I work on the window as the demons lash and claw at the barrier. It covers all of us except Kirilli, who was too far away and has been cut off, swamped by the army of demonic warriors. It's a powerful shield, impervious to physical assault. If the demons continue to hurl themselves at it, they won't inflict any damage and we'll be out of here in another couple of–

"Stand aside!" Lord Loss yells, blasting his way through a pack of gibbering beasts. He studies the barrier and sneers, then howls a phrase of magic. Energy crackles in all eight of his hands. He lets it build, then directs it at the barrier, a stream of sizzling, purple power. Lord Loss is a demon master, far superior to any human in the ways of magic.

Nothing should be able to stand against him. But we're the Kah-Gash and I sense within seconds that we're stronger than our foe. I laugh confidently. We're going to walk out of this without even a scratch. I can't wait to see the look on his face when…

Juni lays a hand on Lord Loss's lumpy flesh. She's changed a lot since I last saw her, become a mutated, flesh-dripping, impossibly ugly beast. Her eyes flare with shocking madness and naked hate. I remember when, as Nadia Moore, she saved my life. She'd committed herself to Lord Loss by that stage, but there was still room in her heart for human feelings.

Not any more. She's become that which she once fought, every bit as heartless as a true child of the Demonata. She screeches vilely and unleashes a burst of magic at the barrier. At her cry, demons huddle around the pair and link with them, adding their energy to hers and Lord Loss's, focusing their combined forces on the shield.

"Grubbs!" Bec pants, feeling the barrier give. "We need more power."

"I can't," he gasps, sweating as we all are, buckling under the strain. "This is as far… as I dare unleash it. If I give it more freedom… I won't be able to control it. Anything could… happen."

I don't understand what he's saying. He must be mad. The barrier will break and they'll be on us in seconds. We have to throw everything we have at them or else we're doomed.

Then I remember when we last gave the Kah-Gash absolute freedom. It drove the universes back in time. If we could count on it working in our favour again, there'd be no need to worry. But we don't know what it will do if we set it loose a second time. Maybe it would give us the strength to defeat the demons — or maybe it would wipe out our universe and hand victory to the Demonata. We dare not play that card unless all else is lost. Our situation is desperate, but not hopeless, and until that changes, Grubbs is right to hold back.

"We have to fight," he roars. "Are you ready?" I nod weakly. "Bec?"

"Go for it," she growls.

With a battle-hungry cry, Grubbs explodes the barrier. A wall of energy spreads like a ripple from a nuclear explosion, flattening the demons closest to us. For a few seconds we're standing at the centre of a clear circle, confusion reigning all around. Then the demons further back recover, bellow brutally and push forward, clambering over the bodies of the fallen, to surround and enclose us.

The real fight begins.

→It's wilder than any battle I've ever been involved in. I've laughed in the face of overwhelming odds before, but nobody's laughing now. There are too many of them, demons of every rank, from familiars up to masters like Lord Loss. All they share is a total hatred of us and a determination to strip our flesh from our bones.

We strike without pause, bolts and fireballs of magic. Hundreds perish within seconds, but still they press on, thousands of fresh monsters to replace each that falls.

I try to stay in touch with Bec and Grubbs, but we're forced apart. Grubbs is dragged away by several demons at least five times his size. A winged beast snatches Bec from the ground and shoots into the air with her.

I go down under the feet of dozens of hard-shelled demons. Claws slash, fangs and pincers snap. I feel rips open down my legs and arms, across my stomach and chest. I ignore the pain, use magic to numb the worst of it, and with a great effort thrust off the demons. Yelling, I stagger to my feet, then collapse again beneath a dinosaur-shaped beast.

Fangs lock around my throat and tighten. I turn the flesh of my neck to steel but the fangs continue to grind together. This is the end. There's nothing I can do. Some wounds are fatal, no matter how magical you are. Once my throat's been crushed, I'm as dead as—

A silver, purple-tipped spike pokes sharply through the centre of the dinosaur's head. It squeals, then falls aside. A panting Dervish pulls me to my feet. The spikes on his head have tripled in length and writhe like snakes, independently of each other, jabbing at the demons around us, driving them back.

"How much longer will it take you to open that bloody window?" he roars.

I look for the patches of light. They're twenty feet away, drifting apart. With a curse, I summon them, pat the stray patches into place and start adding new lights to the pack.

"How long?" Dervish screams again, blood flowing from a chunk that's been bitten out of the left side of his chest — I see snapped white bones poking through the streams of red.

"Maybe a minute," I gasp, hands blurring.

I glance around as I'm putting the window together. Grubbs is back on his feet, supported by his retinue of werewolves, who've torn into the demons around him, attacking rabidly, tearing strips out of their foes. Bec is still fighting with the winged demon and has forced it towards the ground. Meera's close by, doggedly working her way back to us. Her left arm's been severed at the shoulder. Half her face is a clawed-up, blood-soaked mess — her beauty's been spoiled forever. But more worrying than that are the guts dangling from a hole in her stomach, and the small demon wrapped around her waist, tugging at the intestines, reeling them out like a cat unravelling a ball of string.

"Meera!" I scream, desperate to help, but needing to stay focused on the window. It's our only hope of escape. If I abandon it, we're all doomed.

Dervish has spotted Meera too. He begins to dart to her rescue, then swears and drives back a multi-eyed monster that was about to snap off my hands. He has to stand guard. I can't protect myself while I'm working on the window. He's tied to his post, as I am. He weeps with frustration as he fights off the hordes clustered around us, muttering Meera's name over and over.

The demon working on Meera's guts sticks its head into the hole in her stomach. It's giggling sickeningly, like a child tucking into a box of treats. But then its head explodes and it topples to the ground. A figure breaks through the demons around Meera and hauls her forward, towards us. I think my eyes are playing tricks, but when I blink and see the same thing, I realise I'm not dreaming.

Kirilli Kovacs is ploughing through the ranks of demons. One of his hands has turned into a steel scythe and he's mowing down all who come too close. He's the one who rescued Meera.

"Kovacs, you lunatic!" Dervish yells with delight. "You're supposed to be a coward!"

"I am!" Kirilli screeches.

"Then what the hell are you doing?"

"I don't know! I think I'm saving the day! It feels–"

A demon sweeps Kirilli's legs from under him. He flies into the air with a yelp, then is knocked sideways by a bellowing, half-human beast intent on getting her hands on us before any of the others finish us off. Juni Swan is back in the thick of the action.

She angles for Dervish, dripping flesh as she charges, swiping demons out of her way, teeth bared, eyes rolling madly. With a welcoming grunt, Dervish sets his feet firmly and snarls, losing interest in all the other monsters, forgetting his duty to protect me. As Juni rushes him, he grabs hold of her arms and swings her around like an adult whirling a baby. Juni spits acid into his face. He neutralises it swiftly but not before a wide swathe of his flesh bubbles away. The pair fall to the ground, wrestling savagely, stabbing, biting, punching and spitting, each hell-bent on murdering the other.

The window's almost fully formed, but there's no one to watch my back now. Several hound-like demons press tight around me, snapping at my face, digging channels in my flesh with their jagged claws. "Grubbs! Bec!" I scream, turning from the window to drive back the demons. "I need help!"

Grubbs roars at his werewolves. Slipping free of the giants, they struggle towards me, blasting and chewing a path through the packed ranks of monsters.

In the air, Bec's seen off the challenge of the winged demon, but Lord Loss has hit the scene. The pair tumble and roll around overhead. Half his arms are holding her rigidly against his rancid flesh. The other half are lashing her, pulling her hair, trying to gouge out her eyes, digging into her soft flesh.

Meera's in bad shape, but she shoves fistfuls of guts back into the hole in her stomach and dives to Dervish's rescue, pulls Juni Swan off him and scratches at the traitor's eyes. Juni screeches and tries to knock her away, but Meera's stronger than she looks, and she loves Dervish as much as Juni hates him. Grabbing hold of Juni's bloated, rotten head, she jerks her hard and they spin away. Dervish tries to follow, but gets tangled up with another demon.

Grubbs and the few surviving werewolves make it to my side. They're all badly wounded, but they fight as viciously as ever. As they form a half-wall around me, Grubbs yells at me to finish the window and I hurry to obey. The fingers of my left hand have been crushed, but I can still manipulate the patches. Sobbing with pain and fear, I slot one after another into place, praying for the lights to gel and the window to open before it's too late.

Juni's laughing. She's got both hands inside the hole in Meera's stomach and is forcing them up through the layers of guts that still remain, seeking to crush lungs, the heart... whatever she can find.

"Meera!" Dervish howls, trying to force his way through to her but failing.

Meera smiles painfully. She's got her arms wrapped around Juni, holding tight. As Juni tears at Meera's insides, the Disciple catches our gaze and winks wearily. "No... Shadow," she wheezes.

"What's that?" Juni roars.

"No... Shadow," Meera repeats. "When I die... I'm finished... and so... are you."

Juni's face freezes. She catches on to Meera's plan a second too late. Her eyes widen with alarm as she tries to detach herself and dart to safety. But before she can, Meera explodes. She must have been working on the ball of energy since she realised she was beyond help. It bursts from her in a blazing flash of light, shatters her bones, incinerates her flesh — and rips through the mutated, twisted form that Juni built for herself when Death restored her soul to life.

Juni's final howl is lost in the noise of the explosion. She's torn to shreds along with Meera and both women fall to the ground in ragged, bloody, lifeless chunks, their souls freed or lost, however you choose to look at it. Meera has gone to the great beyond, which is a sickening blow. But I experience a burst of joy as well as sorrow, because Juni Swan has perished too and this time no power in the universe can bring the vindictive harpy back. We're rid of her at last!

# CASUALTIES OF WAR

→It sounds like the entire universe is screaming. Dervish and Grubbs wail for Meera. In the air, Lord Loss bellows Juni's name and reaches out to her with a couple of his arms, offering Bec a brief respite. The demon hordes screech with delight, the scent of human death like a red rag to a bull. They press even tighter around us, each wanting to be next to claim a soul.

I drown out the screams and focus on the window. It's all that matters now. We have seconds to get the hell out of here, or we'll wind up like Meera. No time for misery or joy. Just focus, work fast and pray.

A werewolf is slaughtered and collides with me as it thrashes in its death throes, opening a new, deep cut down the side of my head, just behind my left ear. I shrug it off and concentrate.

Kirilli leaps high into the air, raining handfuls of bone down upon the demons. He must have picked them up from the floor of the battlefield. They strike like shrapnel, blinding, wounding, killing. He roars with delight — then shrieks as a demon's jaws flash and his right foot is bitten off at the ankle. Kirilli collapses. His foot drops on top of me and I head it away like a football, never pausing, right hand moving mechanically, fending off demons with my damaged left hand.

Grubbs headbutts a demon and smashes its skull to pieces. His forehead comes out drenched in brains and foul-smelling fluid. Extending his tongue, he licks his eyes clean and fights on, laughing through his tears.

Lord Loss and Bec crash to earth, then rise again. They're still struggling with each other, but he doesn't seem to be inflicting as much damage. His hands move lazily, more like they're caressing Bec than savaging her. And she doesn't react as violently as before. She wriggles less frantically in his embrace, almost as if...

Before I can complete the thought, a window of pale blue light blinks into existence. I stare at it stupidly. Then exhilaration sweeps through me and I yell at the top of my voice. "*The window is open!*"

The Demonata scream hatefully and lash at us frantically. The smarter beasts try to crowd around the window, to block our path, but they're hampered by the mass of demons. There are too many of the monsters. They get in each other's way.

Kirilli hops to the window, grabs Dervish's right

arm – he's still staring at the spot where Meera fell – and topples through, dragging Dervish after him.

A bloodied, panting Grubbs draws up beside me. He casually repels a handful of demons with one swipe of a massive arm. We're both looking to the sky overhead where Bec is locked in the embrace of Lord Loss.

"Go!" she yells. "Leave me!"

"We can't," Grubbs croaks.

"We must," I mutter as more demons bear down on us, snarling, spitting, claws and fangs at full stretch.

"But–" Grubbs begins.

"We're demon fodder if we stay," I snap, then throw myself through the window and out of the demonic universe of death.

→I hit a hard floor and I'm on my feet a split-second later. This is the cave where Beranabus and I were based before our quest to find the Shadow began. It was the first place that popped into my mind when I started putting a window together.

I rip at the fabric of the window, dismantling it, not waiting for Grubbs. If he crosses within the next few seconds, fine. If not, he's a fool and he'll deserve all he gets.

As my hands move within the panel of light, tearing at the individual patches, a werewolf stumbles through, wrapped in the arms of a giant insect-shaped demon. They crash past me and continue their fight on the floor. As Kirilli yelps and slips out of their way, Grubbs backs through the window, bolts of magic flying from his fists, roaring a challenge at those he's leaving behind.

Two more werewolves follow their leader into the cave. The head and shoulders of a third appear, but something clutches its legs and hauls it back. It howls and kicks at whatever has hold. Grubbs grabs the creature and pulls. But then the window comes undone. The patches of light pulse and snap free of each other. The panel vanishes and the werewolf's cut neatly in half, its lower body stranded in the universe of the Demonata, its head and upper arms dropping to the floor here. Its death roar catches in its throat.

It's over.

Well... almost. The insect demon gibbers and breaks free. It darts at the place where the window was, pauses when it realises it's trapped, then turns on me. Before it can strike, all three werewolves pounce. They rip it to pieces and feast on the brittle remains, instantly forgetting about the trauma of the battle, fully focused on their meal, ignoring the rest of us as we sink to the floor and stare silently at each other with shock, bewilderment and dismay.

→Grubbs is the first to move. Rising slowly, groaning

painfully, he hobbles over to check on Dervish. His uncle's in bad shape, the worst of any of us. Blood is pumping from the hole in his chest and I don't think any amount of magic will stop it. Grubbs starts arguing with him. He wants to open a window back to the demon universe, where Dervish will stand a chance of recovery, but the battered Disciple is having none of it. He told Grubbs a while ago that he wanted to die on Earth when his time came. It looks like he'll soon be granted his wish.

"How's the foot?" I ask Kirilli, who's sitting nearby, staring at the place where his right foot used to be. He's crying softly.

"It's gone," Kirilli moans, then looks up. "I don't feel any pain."

"You will soon," I tell him. "But I can work some magic here. I'll bandage it up and help numb the pain. Then I'll open a window and drop you off at a hospital before I leave."

Kirilli doesn't ask where I'm going. Instead he grins weakly. "I did good, didn't I?" he asks hopefully.

"You did great," I smile.

"I never thought I'd be a hero," he whispers. "I dreamt of it many times but I never believed..." He falls silent, reliving the highlights, conveniently ignoring the part where he danced like a fool in the stomach of the Shadow. I don't remind him of that, but fetch bandages from behind the spot where I used to sleep. He's earned the right to be proud. It's not stumbling along the way that matters, but how you finish.

Grubbs limps over as I'm bandaging Kirilli's ankle and healing it with magic, closing off the veins and arteries. He watches silently until I'm done, then nods at me. Leaving Kirilli, we squat near the place where we once kept a fire burning. Grubbs's face has altered. He looks more human than he did when he was fighting. He also looks like he's in a lot of pain, but he says nothing of it.

"Meera's dead," he mumbles.

"I know."

"She took Juni with her. I'd have rather killed that traitor myself, but as long as she's gone..." He sighs, then says quietly, "Dervish is dying. He asked me to take him up top, so he can die outside. I need you to open the trapdoor."

We're deep beneath the ground. A rope ladder leads to the surface, but a stone slab blocks the way out. It's operated by magic. Focusing, I mutter the correct phrase and set it sliding free. "Done."

"Thanks," Grubbs says and starts to rise.

"I could take him to hospital with Kirilli," I suggest.

Grubbs shakes his head. "No point. They couldn't do anything for him. What a moron, letting the demons bite a chunk out of his chest. He should have kept his guard up. The old fool deserves..." He shudders, fighting hard to hold back tears.

"I'll wait for you to return," I tell him.

"That's OK. Take care of Kirilli. You can come back for me."

"I'm not coming back."

Grubbs had made it to his feet, but now he pauses, stares at me and squats again. "What are you talking about?" he asks gruffly.

"It's over. I'm going to the ark."

"You can't. We need you. This isn't finished."

"Of course it is." I wipe blood and sweat from my forehead. I feel so weary. It will be a relief to leave this world and the fighting behind. "We gave it our best shot. We tore the Shadow to pieces. But you heard Beranabus. Death will return, and it'll be even stronger next time. We can't defeat it."

"We have to try," Grubbs growls. "We got the better of it once — we can beat it again. I'll unleash more of the power of the Kah-Gash next time."

"How?" I snort. "We don't have Bec. It's just you and me now."

"We'll rescue her," Grubbs says as if it's the simplest thing in the world. "Lord Loss won't kill her. He'll want to torment her first. I'm guessing he'll return to his kingdom to wait for the Shadow, and he'll take her with him."

"What if he does?" I sigh. "We can't fight him there. We'd stand no chance of defeating a demon master on his home turf."

"Maybe not," Grubbs agrees curtly, "but we have to *try*. Everyone's depending on us. Meera died for this. Dervish will be dead soon too. Beranabus and Bill-E. All the others who've given their lives. They can't have died for nothing. We fight on until the demons kill us all. Only then do we stop."

I shake my head. "If I stay here and perish, the demons will conquer the universe completely. I shouldn't have come back at all, but I did, for one last stab at success. We tried and failed. The ark is all that's left."

I reach out and squeeze Grubbs's arm. "Come with me. They'll welcome you. You can help us keep the ark safe from demons, ensure it never falls to Lord Loss and his stinking kind. It's the best we can do. Staying here is pointless. The fight has moved on. We have to move with it."

"Abandon our world?" Grubbs sneers. "Leave Bec in the clutches of Lord Loss? Run while the demons are weak? Never! They've lost their master. The army will split. They'll fight with each other and return to their own realms. We can harry them, hit hard, drive the fear of the Kah-Gash into them. This isn't the end — it's the beginning. We have the advantage. Now's the time to press it home and make sure that even if Death does return, it has no army to support it."

"That won't work," I say impatiently. "Death's stronger than us, and it's eternal. No matter what we do, it will rise again, recruit new followers and lead them to victory. It's over."

I stand and roll my neck. I want to sleep so badly. But I'll wait until I find Raz, then sleep as we travel to the ark. Forcing off the waves of pain and weariness, I focus on the lights in the air around me and think about Raz in the chamber on Atlantis. As patches blink, I start the long, laborious job of piecing them together.

"That's it?" Grubbs grunts. "You're just going to leave us?"

"It will take several hours to open the window. I'll be here when you get back. You can decide then if you want to come with me or–"

"What about Kirilli?"

I wince. "Damn. I forgot." The stage magician is resting, eyes closed, breathing heavily. I let thoughts of Raz slip from my head and think about a hospital instead. It only takes a few minutes to open this window. When it's ready, I ask Grubbs if he'll help me carry Kirilli through.

"Leave it to me," he says, then picks up the wounded Disciple, slings him over his shoulder like a slab of meat and steps through before the groggy Kirilli has a chance to say goodbye.

While Grubbs is gone, I think about what I'm going to say when he returns. I have to warn him about Bec, tell him what the Old Creature cautioned. I recall the way Lord Loss eased up on her and I realise why I felt so troubled. It looked like they were going to stop fighting, as if she'd said something to make peace with him. Could she have betrayed us like Nadia did? I need to alert Grubbs to the threat before he races after her. Maybe she doesn't want to be rescued. Maybe she's on *their* side now.

As I'm trying to decide where Bec's loyalties lie, Grubbs steps back through the window. I prepare myself to argue with him again, but he smiles and waves my protests away before I can voice them.

"You're right," he chuckles. "You have to go. I wasn't thinking straight."

I sigh with relief. "Will you come with me?" I'm hoping he says yes. Accepting my role on the ark will be hard. It would be a lot easier if I didn't have to face it alone.

"My place is here," he says. "Dervish, Bec, Shark… those are the people I care about. I don't give a stuff about other worlds. I'll fight and I'll die, and if that's not enough, at least I'll have done all that I could. That's what matters most, isn't it, doing all you can, regardless of the consequences?"

"Yes." I smile and extend a hand. "No hard feelings?"

"None," Grubbs says, taking my hand in one of his huge, hairy paws. His smile fades. "But *you* might have some."

I frown curiously. Grubbs is gripping my hand tightly. "What do you–"

Before I can complete the question, Grubbs slashes at my face with his other hand. The sharp, bloody, jagged nails that he was gutting demons with just minutes earlier carve my left eye open. As it pops and I howl with shock and agony, he sweeps his hand back in the opposite direction and rips my right eye out. Then he lets me go.

I fall to the floor screaming, and blindly try to scoop the contents of my ruined eyes back into their sockets.

"I didn't enjoy that," Grubbs says, his words only barely penetrating my veil of screams. "But you agreed – *regardless of the consequences*. I need you, Kernel. I can't fight on without you. So you're staying. End of story."

"My eyes!" I bellow, lashing out furiously, hoping to strike him dead. "Give me back my eyes, you son of a–"

"Can't," Grubbs says calmly. "But what I will do,

once I'm done with Dervish and we've had time to patch up our wounds, get our breath back and link up with support troops, is open a window back to the universe of the Demonata. You'll be able to build another pair of eyes there. And then you'll use them to find Bec and help me rescue her."

"You're mad!" I holler, swinging for him again. "Come here so I can kill you!"

"There'll be plenty of time for killing," Grubbs says, backing away. "Forget your crazy ark. I'm your keeper now. All other bets are off."

"Come back!" I yell, stumbling after him and falling. "You don't know what you're doing. You're handing victory to them. We can't trust Bec. She'll betray us. Lord Loss will be waiting. Death will..."

I stop. I've been shouting to myself. I can hear Grubbs scrabbling up the rope ladder with Dervish, ignorant of my cries. Apart from the werewolves, which are still snacking on the insect demon's remains, I'm alone.

Abandoned and blind, I strike the floor pitifully, then moan softly and lower my face into the blood and dust, wishing the roof would cave in and finish me off. If I still had eyes, I'd weep, not for myself, but for the multitudes of creatures who'll have nowhere to hide when their worlds burn.

"What the hell have we done?" I sob.

*All that you could*, I imagine the voice of Beranabus whispering. And then, after a short, bitter pause, he adds with a sarcastic chuckle, *But it wasn't enough. This universe is finished. Goodnight, Vienna!*

BOOK TEN OF **THE DEMONATA**

Don't miss the Earth-shattering conclusion, coming October 2009

www. darrenshan.com

BOOK ONE OF **THE DEMONATA**

When Grubbs Grady first encounters Lord Loss and his evil minions, he learns three things:

- the world is vicious,
- magic is possible,
- demons are real.

He thinks that he will never again witness such a terrible night of death and darkness.

...He is wrong.

*Also available on audio, read by Rupert Degas*

PB ISBN 0 00 719320 3
CD ISBN 0 00 721389 1

# DARREN SHAN
# THE DEMON THIEF

BOOK TWO OF **THE DEMONATA**

When Kernel Fleck's brother is stolen by demons, he must enter their universe in search of him. It is a place of magic, chaos and incredible danger. Kernel has three aims:

- learn to use magic,
- find his brother,
- stay alive.

But a heartless demon awaits him, and death has been foretold…

*Also available on audio, read by Rupert Degas*

PB ISBN 0 00 719323 8
CD ISBN 0 00 722977 1

BOOK THREE OF **THE DEMONATA**

Nightmares haunt the dreams of Dervish Grady since his return from the Demonata universe, but Grubbs takes care of his uncle as they both try to continue a normal, demon-free existence. When a legendary cult director calls in Dervish as consultant for a new horror movie, it seems a perfect excuse for a break from routine and a chance for some fun. But being on the set of a town called Slawter stirs up more than memories for Grubbs and his friend Bill-E.

*Also available on audio, read by Rupert Degas*

HB ISBN 0 00 722955 0
CD ISBN 0 00 722978 X

BOOK FOUR OF **THE DEMONATA**

As a baby, Bec fought for her life. As a trainee priestess, she fights to fit in to a tribe that needs her skills but fears her powers. And when the demons come, the fight becomes a war.

Bec's magic is weak and untrained, until she meets the druid Drust. Under his leadership, Bec and a small band of warriors embark on a long journey through hostile lands to confront the Demonata at their source. But the final conflict demands a sacrifice too horrific to contemplate…

*Also available on audio, read by Lorraine Pilkington*

PB ISBN 978 0 00 723139 3
CD ISBN 978 0 00 722979 6

BOOK FIVE OF **THE DEMONATA**

Grubbs Grady has so far escaped the family curse, but when he begins to experience alarming symptoms at the onset of the full moon, he is scared that the jaws of fate are opening and about to swallow him whole.

He has cheated death, defeated demons, moved on with his life. But Grubbs is torn between the world of magic and his wolfen genes. Can he fight the beast inside or will he fall victim to his tainted blood?

*Also available on audio, read by Rupert Degas*

PB ISBN 978 0 00 723140 9
CD ISBN 978 0 00 722980 2